Love Scenes

Where romance and excitement take center stage

FACE THE MUSIC

Simone Nicholas

BALLANTINE BOOKS • NEW YORK

All rights reserved under International and Pan-American
Copyright Conventions. Published in the United States of
America by Ballantine Books, a division of Random House,
Inc., New York, and simultaneously in Canada by Random
House of Canada Limited, Toronto.

Library of Congress Catalog Card Number: 86-91594

ISBN 0-345-33241-5

Printed in Canada

First Edition: March 1987

✳ 1 ✳

FRANCESCA HESITATED ON THE TOP STEP OF MacCREADY Hall, and looked slowly around at her new home. She was going to be late. It was already five to two and the note in the welcoming package on her dorm room door said to be at the Dewey Theater of the Arthur J. Kenner Performing Arts Center no later than two o'clock for the introductory assembly. But still she hesitated. She hadn't had time to catch her breath, to think about all this day really meant. Now, staring across the ancient, stately campus of Lowell College with its impressive ivy-covered brick walls and towering trees, it hit her full force. Her large, deep-set dark eyes stung with tears. For the first time in her life, she was on her own. Really alone. Even as a kid when she'd spent summers away at the music camp in Vermont, she'd been surrounded by her talented brothers and sisters, who had also attended. Francesca desperately tried to will away the nagging stomachache that had been with her since early morning.

But, she thought, taking a deep, shaky breath, being in Lowell, Connecticut, at least meant one good thing. ̇ were almost two hundred miles between her and Da

She wished it were two thousand! Two million! She couldn't have faced him at school again this year. The memories were still too vivid, the sense of embarrassment too raw.

The confusion of that night came back now full force. Had she meant to lead him on? Had she asked for it? What had she wanted? To break all the rules her father ever set for her; to make her first independent stand? Or was she really—behind her controlled, proper facade—just like the girls she'd been warned about. Girls who could push her into a faster crowd. Girls who invited boys, just by the look in their eyes, to touch. . . .

Francesca shuddered unhappily and pulled her jacket tighter around her, forcing the nightmare back into the far recesses of her mind, where she had tried desperately to keep it stored since last spring. Slowly the campus of Lowell College came back into focus. Yes, she was glad to be here, thankful she'd been accepted into SPAR— Students in Performing Arts Repertory—one of the most accelerated and prestigious programs for high school theater students in the country. But maybe she should have followed the advice in the SPAR handbook and arrived last night—Saturday. The morning had been such a rush, with her train from Boston leaving late and getting hung up in New Haven, and now she'd missed the eleven o'clock registration and would have to go to a special session at five. She hated the thought that the advanced voice class— vocal interpretation—might be full. It sounded like a lot of fun . . . and very sophisticated.

Francesca slowly descended the worn stone steps of MacCready Hall. Suddenly, two boys and a girl burst through the door behind her and dashed past, obviously in a hurry. Francesca stared after them. Her SPAR pamphlets had said MacCready was a coed dorm, with the boys and girls on alternating floors. The very thought of it unnerved Francesca. She forced herself to concentrate on the surroundings.

The day was crisp and sunny with an early September breeze fluttering through the silvery beech trees and pushing a few prematurely dried leaves across the beautifully manicured lawns between the imposing Gothic buildings. The breeze toyed with Francesca's hair, gently picking up a strand and waving it, then another and another until it formed a swirling mass like a slow-motion, nighttime sea around her head and down her back. In contrast, her face seemed even paler than usual, the features more delicate, yet intense. Francesca sunk her hands deep in the pockets of her baggy linen trousers and let her eyes wander back and forth trying to take it all in, trying to understand that this was home for the next year.

It is beautiful here, she admitted to herself with a sigh before heading up a path that led from the dorm in the middle of the hill to the main campus at the top. The buildings up here were formally arranged with connecting broad brick pathways between them. Numerous iron and hardwood benches dotted the hill under the huge, ancient trees, giving the whole scene an unhurried, parklike air. It felt orderly and proper and right . . . like Boston . . . home.

Beyond this formal setting, almost hidden in a copse of dogwood trees that were already starting to turn red, sat a little stone church, looking for all the world like an enchanted house in a magic forest. It was all knobbly and funny angles and friendly. Steps led down from this highest point on the campus to the new section of the school at the bottom. Francesca could see what had to be the cafeteria—a long, low building with a flagstone patio filled with modern black tables and chairs, a striking contrast to the stately old school.

Consulting her map of the campus and looking just beyond the cafeteria, Francesca felt her heart race anew. Nestled into the side of the hill, its lower floor almost buried in a sea of rhododenron, was the Arthur J. Kenner

Performing Arts Center, the hub of her world for the next year. It was huge and impressive—a modern oasis of pink granite and smoked glass that seemed to float like an exotic plant in its woodland setting. And knowing it housed some of the finest accommodations for theater classes and stage productions in New England made it even more impressive. There were two separate theaters, and numerous dance studios, as well as music and lecture rooms. What a luxury! At Newton High back in Boston, the theater students were always forced to share the tiny stage with every other club or organization that put in a bid for it. Here it would be all theater!

As Francesca approached the arts center, she experienced a powerful, clear rush of fear. She was one of only a hundred applicants out of thousands across the country to be accepted for this famous theater arts program. But what if she didn't measure up? She knew she had talent. After all, hadn't she won just about every voice competition in the northeast for high school kids? But here she was going to be up against her toughest competition yet. She'd have to prove herself every day. She'd have to commit herself like she never even imagined committing herself before. Did she have the stamina? Did she have what it took to succeed?

Francesca wished her roommate had been around so they could have gone to this first assembly together . . . even though she had the distinct feeling that they couldn't be more different people. Her roommate had been in evidence only by a huge duffel bag with "Eve Jacobson" scrawled across it and a knapsack and several tennis rackets dumped confidently in the middle of the floor and on both beds. This alone made Francesca nervous. It reminded her of people she knew back home—the crowd she never completely felt a part of. Francesca had parked her own leather luggage neatly in the corner, afraid to claim any part of the room for herself. They'd have to work that out later.

Suddenly two boys came racing out the door, almost knocking Francesca over. The lean black boy grinned broadly at Francesca.

"Hey, you're going to catch some kind of mean bug standing around with your mouth open like that." He smiled. His friend's large blue eyes traveled appreciatively over Francesca's graceful figure. Francesca froze, unsure of what to say or do.

"You must be with SPAR," she finally managed, moments later. Then she cringed. It sounded so dumb.

"Right you are!" chanted the black boy, twirling around with astounding ease on sneakered feet. Francesca tried to suppress a giggle, but failed. What a neat guy.

"I'm Clive," he said, bowing dramatically, "and this is my main man—Michael."

Suddenly Clive jumped back and, looking Francesca up and down, exclaimed, "With those long legs, you must be a dancer, too."

Francesca felt her face go bright red. "I've studied ballet," she offered softly. It unnerved her to be stared at like that. It reminded her . . . No, she didn't want to be reminded again today. Ever! Damian was far away. It was time to forget him, forget the nightmare . . . if she could.

She quickly explained that she was a singer and actress, omitting the fact that she had little confidence in her stage work. . . . Francesca had never felt comfortable acting, although she'd been in quite a few school plays. Hopefully, this year at SPAR would give her the skills she needed. Singing was a lot, but it wasn't everything.

"Aren't we supposed to be at some sort of assembly?" she asked, easing the subject away from herself.

"Five minutes ago," said Clive, glancing at his watch.

"Let's move out," added Michael, doing a simple but beautifully executed tap dance over the back of a nearby bench, then heading off toward Kenner. Taking a deep breath, Francesca hurried off after the boys. It was time, she told herself defiantly, ''to face the music.'' Just for a moment she laughed out loud. It was only an expression, but it felt so ridiculously accurate. . . .

❋ 11 ❋

FRANCESCA PUSHED THROUGH THE HUGE, TINTED-GLASS doors of Kenner behind the boys and joined the other students milling nervously around in anticipation of the first assembly. Many of them were gathered around a large sign that had been taped onto a wall. Self-consciously Francesca eased her way over to the group and studied the announcement.

SONG & DANCE TALENT CONTEST

Come one, come all to the first talent contest

of many.

Friday night, September 28

Dewey Theater 8 PM

Fifteen Volunteer Competitors Needed

Sign Up below

Francesca swallowed hard and looked around. There wasn't a single name on the sign-up sheet and no one had pen in hand. For a crazy moment she considered being the

first. She could always rely on her voice. But a second
glance around the room brought a change of heart. Who
were these kids anyway? They could be so talented that in
comparison she would look like nothing. How could she
take that chance? Quickly, Francesca moved away from the
contest announcement. Sooner or later she would have to
participate, but a mere three weeks from now just wasn't
the time.

People were talking and laughing in groups of twos and
threes and almost immediately Francesca heard a voice
distinguish itself from the others.

"Minelli! For heaven's sake!" came the thick southern
accent, wrapping itself around the group like warm honey.

Startled at hearing her name called out, Francesca turned
her attention to a tall, strikingly beautiful girl who was
scrutinizing a list of names posted on the bulletin board
outside the Harriet T. Dewey Theater. As the girl leaned
closer to the list, her shank of rich auburn hair slid heavily
forward around her shoulders. Without missing a beat, she
flicked it back with a practiced toss of her head. It spread
out across the large black-and-red checks of her oversize
jacket like an expensive shawl, every strand magically in
place.

"Look! Right here! It says Minelli! Room 303 MacCready
Hall."

"Room 303! Wow! That's my room! You mean Minelli's
my roommate?"

With curiosity and apprehension, Francesca watched a
short, energetic girl—her roommate—push to the front of
the crowd gathering with interest around the list. She
shoved big tortoiseshell glasses back up on her nose and
squinted at the names.

"Maybe she'd get me an introductin to Vincente Minelli.
What an in! What a break!"

"Can it, Jacobson," shouted someone teasingly from
the crowd. "What would a great director want with you?"

A few people laughed, but Francesca didn't join in. She could see the pain in Eve's face. Still it puzzled her. Eve didn't look like the sensitive type, and the comment had obviously been meant as a joke.

"Hey . . . I'm a good director," Eve shot back defensively. "He might take me on as an assistant or something."

"How about stage sweeper?" someone else quipped.

Francesca glanced uneasily at the group out of the corner of her eye. People were still filtering in, and watching them greet each other familiarly made Francesca feel even more alone. Most of these kids had arrived the evening before and shared dinner together. Now, one Sunday breakfast, registration, and lunch later, they'd had the chance to get to know each other before this first assembly.

She looked back at Eve, wondering if she ought to go over and introduce herself so they could sit together; there was nothing worse than walking into a room full of strangers. But already she was sure that she and her roommate were entirely different sorts of people; the memory of the sporty knapsack and tennis racket collection returned. Eve seemed so self-assured—physically. Her own schedule of violin and voice lessons since early childhood had left her with only enough time to be envious of people who could rush at a tennis ball and whack it energetically across the net, or take off into the mountains with only a sack of provisions on their backs.

Francesca eyed Eve's compact, neat body. Short people always made her feel insecure. They could just kind of sneak through life without calling a lot of attention to themselves. Francesca didn't like the feeling, at five-foot-nine, of always being on show, like a giraffe or something. She wondered why SPAR's directors had put her in with someone who was obviously her opposite. When she'd filled out her application describing herself and her interests, she'd thought it was so they could match her with a roommate of similar interests. No such luck, it seemed.

Francesca sighed deeply but inaudibly. She couldn't let
the others see how nervous she was. They all seemed so
mature . . . so . . . professional. Not like the kids she was
used to back home. Well, she wasn't like the kids back
home either, for that matter. She wasn't like anyone. She
wasn't even the girl she thought she was. Hadn't Damian
proven that? She could still feel his hands on her body, his
warm breath on her neck. It had felt so good . . . but so
uncontrollable. She took another deep breath, squared her
shoulders, and forced the memory back down inside. She
was here to study acting and voice, to rise to the top if she
could. That was all she had to think about. Her dark eyes
glowed with determination. Maybe she would sign up for
the talent contest after all. Maybe she'd even win. . . .

Francesca leaned back against the marble column on the
outskirts of the main crowd and studied her new classmates. Suddenly someone tripped over her bag, which had
been resting on the floor.

"I'm sorry," whispered Francesca, then seeing it was
her roommate, she smiled uncertainly. Well, might as well
get it over. They'd have to meet sometime.

"It was my fault," said Eve, looking up at Francesca in
awe. "I'm sorry."

"I think we must be roommates," said Francesca in her
soft voice. "I'm Francesca Minelli."

"You are!" began Eve enthusiastically. "Are you. . . ?"

"No . . . I'm not," interrupted Francesca, feeling very
uncomfortable as she watched Eve's face fall, the smile
disappear. Why did she get the feeling she'd just let her
roommate down? This was definitely not a great start to
things.

"Oh well, never mind," continued Eve, brightening.
"It would have just been a great break for me. I'm a
directing student and . . . well . . . an introduction to
Vincente Minelli certainly couldn't hurt the old career, if
you know what I mean."

Francesca was about to answer when a pleasant voice rose above the others from across the hall, where most of the kids were gathered, milling around nervously. Francesca felt like she and Eve were the audience watching a play.

"You don't think she's a real Minelli, do you?" The voice belonged to a girl who looked for all the world like a slightly plump Meryl Streep—open and friendly and non-threatening, but funky at the same time. Francesca loved her neon-pink overalls, and her thick, curly hair cut short at the sides but full and dramatic on top. Francesca decided that, unlike herself, this was a girl with the sophistication to carry off just about any style she chose.

"A real Minelli, as in Liza with a Z and all that?" continued the girl.

"This whole thing is getting out of hand," Francesca said quietly to Eve, starting toward the girl who was talking. Eve grabbed her arm and pulled her back.

"No, hang on a sec," she said, her gray-blue eyes twinkling mischievously. "This could be good."

"I can't let them keep thinking I'm related to *the* Minellis," protested Francesca. Not identifying herself made her feel like she was listening in on someone else's phone conversation. It just didn't seem right.

"Those two are roommates," explained Eve in whispers. "The one with the wild southern accent and I-just-stepped-from-the-pages-of-*Vogue* looks is Iris Setlow, and the other is Ellie Miller. Ellie's great. Really neat. We shared a table at lunch and spent most of the time pretending we were hamburgers and cheeseburgers—you know, trying out our acting skills on each other." Eve giggled. "You should see her do a takeoff of a kosher dill pickle. Unbelievable, I tell you. Wow, can she ever act!"

Francesca giggled, too.

"Anyway, you never saw two such different people,"

continued Eve. "I think they must hate each other the way they're already at each other's throats."

Francesca gave Eve a quick look. What about us? We're about as different as two people can possibly be, she thought. Are we going to be at each other's throats, too?

"Dear Lord," gushed a tall blond girl, breaking away from a group of boys at the water fountain and slinking past Francesca. Her jeans were so tight Francesca thought she could hear them groan in protest at every movement of the willowy body encased inside. Her red high heels echoed noisily across the cavernous space. The looks the boys were giving her as she eased herself beyond their reach brought blood rushing to Eve's face.

"What *is* going on?" continued the blonde.

"Oh, nothing, Se-re-na," said Iris, sarcastically emphasizing every syllable of the name tag on Serena's pocket. "Our humble little group just happens to have a Minelli in its midsts, and . . ." She shot Eve a questioning look across the room.

"Eve . . . Eve Jacobson . . . director," Eve called back firmly, then turned to Francesca and whispered conspiratorially. "I saw Iris in action at lunch. A real Scarlett O'Hara if there ever was one. Geez, you should have seen her going from table to table introducing herself with the phoniest, let's-all-be-friends smile pasted all over her face. Girls like that make me want to throw up—always demanding their 'way' because they think they're so cute and terrific. Yuck!"

"And Eve the Director here just happens to have her as a roommate," continued Iris, never losing her cool as Serena's ice-blue eyes held hers in a cold stare.

Serena was the only one who looked like she totally didn't belong in the group, thought Francesca. Eve whispered in her ear that Serena was from California, but Francesca had already guessed. Although Francesca had never been there, Serena seemed the typical "California

Girl." She was tall with sun-streaked, disheveled blond hair and a permanently healthy, tan glow. Her eyes sparkled with a devil-may-care, bring-on-the-party look.

"She's a singer . . . supposedly," said Eve. "Although she just doesn't look serious enough to be very good, does she?"

"Don't let looks fool you," Francesca heard herself say. Like mine, she wanted to add. She wished she could tell someone what she was really like inside—how trapped she felt by her own desires, the desires that had unleashed something in Damian she wanted, but desperately feared.

"I'm pretty sure Vincente Minelli only has the one daughter, and no sons, so no Minellis our age," said a well-built blond boy of medium height, interrupting Francesca's private nightmare.

"That's C.J. Rollings from Texas," informed Eve in a low voice. "A real Robert Redford, huh? Only trouble is, he knows it. This guy is conceit personified, I tell you. His old man's loaded. Oil. I heard C.J. was flown up here on a private jet. Pretty wild, huh?"

Francesca wasn't attracted to his near perfect looks, but had to agree he was oozing confidence. Watching his smooth control over the group, she wondered what his weak spot was. She'd never seen that kind of self-assurance in a seventeen-year-old.

"I bet this guy's just swarming through on his looks and money," said Eve critically. "Well, I guess this next year will tell. We'll just see how long he lasts. Apparently he got in on his acting, but he sings, too."

Francesca didn't answer. She was watching a pair of warm blue eyes a few feet away dance mischievously under a mop of thick black curls. For a moment they rested on her . . . with obvious interest.

"Marty . . . I can't remember his last name," whispered Eve following the direction of Francesca's gaze. "We shared a limousine from the airport. He's weird."

Francesca glanced at Eve with awe. She'd sure met a lot of their classmates in the few hours they'd all been together. Another difference, thought Francesca with envy. It was going to take her weeks to get to meet even a handful. She just didn't have Eve's confidence. She couldn't just plunge in and introduce herself. She was more the private type.

"Of course, she could be Liza's long-lost sister," said Marty, his Brooklyn twang almost as thick as Iris's southern drawl. He winked at the group and leaned against the wall, pushing his crumpled white shirt back down in his slick-fitting, faded jeans. Francesca swallowed hard and tried to pull her eyes away from the long, sensual lines of his relaxed body. She failed. He wasn't conventionally good looking, not like C.J., but something about him fascinated her . . . as much as it unnerved her. She could sense an energy bubbling within him just below the surface. It scared her . . . and intrigued her to think what form it would take when it bubbled over.

"Maybe you're right," Iris shot back. "Of course, only someone like you would guess at the sordid details about someone else's sex life."

Francesca knew now she had to put a stop to the debate over her name, even if it meant calling attention to herself. Her heart pounded with fear. Taking a few seconds to collect herself, she put on a brave smile, walked over to the group, and faced Iris.

"Hello . . . I'm Francesca Minelli. . . ." she said, trying to keep her voice from shaking.

* III *

"**M**INELLI! YOU'RE MINELLI!?" STAMMERED IRIS, momentarily losing her cool as she looked Francesca over from head to toe. Francesca squirmed uneasily under the intense scrutiny, which seemed to go on forever. When Iris finally took Francesca's outstretched hand in her own limp, cold one, Francesca got the distinct feeling Iris was furious. But why? Surely she's not jealous, thought Francesca with surprise, catching Iris giving her the once over again. No, that was ridiculous. What did Iris have to be jealous of? She was plenty good-looking herself.

"You don't even look like her!" burst out Iris when she finally found her voice again. "You can't be a Minelli!"

Francesca fell back a step. Iris's loud accusation had everyone staring at her. Nervously she fingered the buttons of her denim jacket, wishing she'd left it in her room. The day was warmer than she'd thought.

"Back off, Iris," demanded Ellie, pushing through the crowd. She put her arm around Francesca's shoulders and glared at Iris. "And I thought you southern types prided yourself on good manners."

Ellie turned to Francesca and introduced herself. Francesca smiled her gratitude, feeling herself relax.

"You'll have to excuse Iris, I'm afraid," whispered Ellie, gently directing her away to a corner. "Until you arrived, she was queen of the day, or thought she was, at least. I just hope she doesn't take it out on you."

"Take what out on me?" asked Francesca innocently.

"Oh, the simple little fact that you're the most gorgeous girl here."

Francesca felt her face go beet-red. "Oh, no . . . surely . . . of course not."

"Well, it's true," said Ellie matter-of-factly. "And Iris Setlow's not the type to welcome competition of any sort, especially in that area. Friendly warning—watch out for her. She's a real snake in the grass."

Francesca looked around to give Iris a smile, to try to reassure her that they could be friends, but there was no sign of her.

"Oh . . . uh . . . by the way," began Ellie hesitantly. "We were . . . uh . . . all getting a bit antsy waiting for the assembly to start and got all excited about your last name when we saw it on the list. You're not . . . I mean . . . not really . . . you know . . . related to Liza and all."

Francesca laughed, more with relief than at the absurdity of the thought. "I wish I were, but I'm afraid I've got to disappoint you."

"Well, you certainly don't disappoint me," said C.J., sliding up beside her and smoothly maneuvering her away from Ellie. Francesca looked at him with surprise and swallowed hard. Sure he was gorgeous, but who did he think he was, putting the moves on her like that? She gave him one of the icy stares she'd been practicing over and over for such moments. But she could tell he wasn't convinced. C.J. clearly wasn't used to hearing no, and he was making it painfully obvious. Francesca pulled away just as the door to the Dewey Theater, the smaller of the two theaters in the Kenner Center, opened.

"All rrrrrrrright," whooped Marty. "Let's get this show on the road."

"Okay, kids, take it easy," said the man at the door. The gray flecks in his hair and the lines around his eyes and mouth suggested he must be around forty, but he was in good shape; power and energy radiated from his stocky form. Slowly, with dark eyes staring intently, he looked from one student to the next until he held everyone's gaze.

"I'm ready for you," he said quietly when the group had fallen silent. "Please . . . through here." He motioned to a set of double doors that led into an intimate theater with seats for no more than about two hundred encircling the stage. A real theater-in-the-round, thought Francesca with awe, falling into step with the others and trying to take it all in at once. It was so professional looking, with its sophisticated lighting system hanging from the rafters, and the multispeaker sound system. This was the real thing—all dark and otherworldly like theaters should be. Francesca sank into one of the red velvet seats, oblivious to the others moving into place around her.

It was finally starting. Her big dream. In the next year she would come up against some of the best young theater talent in the country. She looked around, her eyes wide with wonder. Many of these kids would make it, and make it big—all the way to Broadway . . . Hollywood. Would she be one of them? Francesca leaned back her chair and heaved a sigh. The talent show was coming too soon for her. She'd wait for a later competition. She didn't want to find out so early on that talent in Boston did not necessarily mean talent anywhere else. . . .

"Okay, students," came a voice from the front of the auditorium, wresting her attention. The stocky, mysterious man took the podium. "Welcome to SPAR. I'm Zed Andromis, the program director. Please call me Zed. I'll

tell you once that I'm impressed you're here. Only a
hundred of you were picked from thousands of applicants
across the country. You wouldn't be here if you didn't
have talent. But after this, you've got to prove it to me.
You've been accepted into one of the best theater programs in the United States, and it's up to you what you do
with it.''

"What a hunk, huh?" whispered Eve.

"He is cute," giggled Francesca. "Kind of intense,
though, don't you think?"

"I think that's sexy," sighed Eve, without ever turning
her attention away from the stage.

"As you all know, you'll be expected to keep up with
your regular high school academic classes this year. These
will be taught by graduate students in the education program here at Lowell, and I want to emphasize that these
courses are just as important as your theater studies. I
won't tolerate laziness or neglect in any way. I hope you
understand that.''

Francesca glanced around to catch the others' reactions
to Zed's heavy speech. Serena, sitting two seats away,
rolled her eyes and went back to filing her nails. Iris was
searching for split ends in her shampoo-advertisement-
perfect hair. Ellie and Marty were all attention. Francesca's eyes lingered on Marty for an extra moment, then
moved on quickly to C.J. At first he looked like he was
hanging on Zed's every word—he was leaning forward
intently—but Francesca soon noticed that he wasn't even
seeing the stage, merely staring at it, his mind obviously
miles away. His eyes were glazed and looked almost . . .
but it couldn't be . . . not C.J. . . . but yes, it was
definitely there. Fear. Real fear. It was so apparent and so
familiar that it sent a shiver down Francesca's back. Did
C.J. have some secret he kept all to himself . . . like she
had? Francesca dismissed this idea immediately. What

kind of problem could this gorgeous, rich, supposedly talented person have?

"And now for the fun part," continued Zed, pulling her attention back to the stage. "Throughout the year, we'll be putting on a couple of musicals, along with some straight drama and some classic comedies, of course, but I thought we might as well plunge in and choose a musical today. On the bulletin board outside the main theater next door are two sheets labeled *West Side Story* and *Grease*. Please vote for the one you'd like to do first by putting your name underneath. Got that?"

Everyone clapped, Eve the loudest.

"And now I'd like to turn you over to my colleague and your musical director, Lilly Chamberlain," continued Zed.

Francesca clapped politely as a small, slender woman in her fifties gracefully mounted the stage. She inclined her head slightly at Zed in acknowledgment when he handed over the podium, then turned to face her audience.

"I heard she dated Laurence Olivier for a while some years back," whispered Eve.

Francesca's eyes widened and she looked at the little woman with renewed awe. Laurence Olivier! Now, there was a real gentleman. She couldn't imagine him pushing himself on anyone; not like . . . like . . . But then, hadn't it been her own excitement . . . her own . . . passion . . . that had led Damian on? Francesca shoved the thought aside, thankful to be at Lowell College with a year of hard work before her. It would help her forget, help her get away from facing herself before she was ready.

"I don't have much to add," began Lilly, her voice soft and musical but vibrant at the same time, "except to say that Zed's bark is worse than his bite, so don't take him too seriously." She smiled mischievously over at Zed while the group cracked up. Francesca could see that she had been beautiful when she was younger. Her smile still held the power of that beauty, trapped like some precious flower.

"Did you see that smile she gave Zed?" Francesca asked Eve slyly. "Do you think they have something going?"

"Yeah. It looks pretty cozy," Eve whispered back mournfully. "I can't compete with that woman. She's beautiful."

"Oh, Eve, surely you aren't serious about competing, anyway Zed's more than twice your age," said Francesca, surprised to discover the intensity of Eve's attraction.

"I may only be seventeen," said Eve, glancing away, "but I'm much older than my years."

Francesca wanted to laugh. It sounded very melodramatic, but she stifled her giggles when she saw Zed again take the podium. He looked very serious.

"I almost forgot," he began, nodding at Lilly with a soft smile as she stood by his side. "I imagine all of you have seen the talent contest announcement. I want to make it perfectly clear that when I say I want fifteen volunteers, I mean it. I think these competitions are a good way to get you used to critical and maybe even sometimes hostile audiences. There's going to be a contest every three weeks. This one is song and dance. The next is going to be drama. I expect everyone to sign up at least two times this year— and if you don't, I'll do it for you. No one is excluded . . . not even students specializing in directing or stage design."

A soft murmur filled the room as Zed paused. Francesca looked down at her hands. She knew SPAR would be intense, but somehow it was beginning to feel overwhelming. Silently she looked at Eve, but the expression on her roommate's face made her forget her anxieties. Eve was gazing almost lovingly at Zed, her face glowing with adoration. Francesca cringed. It was all too much. She was in over her head. She just wasn't sophisticated enough for any of this. . . .

"Okay, then," Zed continued after a whispered conversation with Lilly, "I'm looking forward to a terrific year. Please file out slowly. We don't need any broken bones now!"

Francesca stood up quickly. The large theater suddenly felt very stuffy. Impatiently, she waited for her row to empty out, and then, Eve close behind, she made her way to the big doors in the back of the theater.

Everyone was clustered around the bulletin board.

"Okay, gang, let's make *West Side Story* our first big hit," called out Marty, signing his name with a flourish on the appropriate sheet moments after the meeting was adjourned.

The others clustered around him outside Thompson Theater, the larger of the two theaters in the Performing Arts Center.

"*West Side Story!*" snapped Eve, signing her own name under *Grease*. "Let's at least do something with a little pizzazz. *West Side Story* is such old hat."

"Old hat, my foot!" Marty retorted. "It's a classic. It's a real tour de force of the stage. And I'm going to direct it."

"Have fun," said Eve coolly. "But *Grease* will be first, and with my direction, it will fly!"

"Not a chance. *Grease* is fluff. Pure fluff. The others will see that," Marty said. "*West Side Story* is a classic. It's timeless—a real challenge to everyone to do their best."

"I suppose that's a typical response from your pea brain," Eve came back, then added sarcastically, " 'A challenge to everyone.' That's rich, Marty. Real rich. Mind if I quote you on that?"

"Since we're going to be doing both musicals anyway," said Francesca, easing into the conversation, "you'll both get your chance. What's the use in arguing?"

Marty shifted his feet uncomfortably, then looked up at Eve with a sheepish grin. "I guess she's right, huh?"

"Yeah," said Eve, her face flushed with embarrassment. "Sorry I flew off the handle like that."

"I started it," Marty came back. "I'm the one who should apologize."

"No, I started it," Eve interrupted. "Remember? I called *West Side Story* 'old hat.' "

"Are you two going to start arguing all over again?" asked Francesca.

Marty and Eve burst out laughing.

And they were still laughing when Marty caught Francesca's eye. He immediately forgot everything else as he turned to study her face. Here was his chance. She couldn't hold it against him to just introduce himself. After all, that's what they were supposed to be doing, wasn't it? This was the first day of the rest of their lives. . . .

* IV *

C. J. SIGNED UP FOR *GREASE*, PENCILING HIS NAME IN beside Francesca's. So what if she'd tried to give him the brush-off earlier. She couldn't resist him forever. No one could. At least no one ever had. He ran a practiced hand through his thick, blond hair—girls liked the rumpled look—and turned back to the group just as Marty headed for Francesca.

"What do you say you and I split this scene and check out the town," said C.J., smoothly cutting Marty off and taking Francesca's arm. She really was gorgeous: reminded him of Nastassia Kinski, his favorite actress. The same deep-set, huge, mysterious eyes that made her seem so vulnerable. And he loved that full, sensuous mouth. It was made for kissing.

He started to put his arm around Francesca's shoulders, but her wide-eyed stare caught him off guard. He hesitated. She's afraid of me, he thought, or is it resentment? No one had ever looked at him like that, but he knew the look. He imagined his own eyes reflected that same stare every time his father took over his life and tried to make things go smoothly by shelling out a few more megabucks and bribing someone else to open doors for his precious son. It was a look of frustration and fear. A look that said "Let me alone."

"I only got here a couple of hours ago," began Francesca in her soft, well-modulated voice, looking at him warily. "I think I ought to meet some of the others."

"Well, let's just invite them all to go with us," C.J. said breezily, quickly regaining his composure. Before she could protest, he announced in a loud voice, "Okay, everyone down to Tony's on Main Street. The pizza's on me."

The loud yell that went up as the gang surged through the doors of Kenner and headed for town warmed C.J.'s heart. He liked to be popular, needed to know people really liked him. He turned to Francesca, but she was gone, walking determinedly away from him. For a moment C.J. hesitated, wondering if he should pursue her. But then he shrugged, and instead increased his pace to catch up with the blonde ahead of him. Francesca could wait. He needed to feel good now.

"Hi, Serena," C.J. said smoothly, draping his arm around her shoulders.

C.J. liked the town of Lowell, or at least what he'd seen of it so far. It was small and quaint; most of the buildings were Victorian, late 1800s, but a few were even older. It was all white clapboard and dark shutters and picket fences. A real little New England town. A class act, he thought. And very homey. Nothing over three stories here, and that was usually one of the big old homes that lined Main Street. Dallas—home—was so big and impersonal, all glass and chrome and glitz, nothing you could get close to—but Lowell kind of begged to be your friend. C.J. liked that. He also liked being two thousand miles away from his father . . . and the Rollings fortune. For the first time in a long time he felt that he could breathe. The fear that his father had bought him his place at SPAR began to disappear. He sucked the sweet autumn air deep into his lungs and squeezed Serena's shoulder. She responded just the way he hoped she would, leaning comfortably in against him.

He led the gang through the park that formed the border between the town and college, and around the edge of the lake in the middle. Beautifully tended grass sloped right down to the edge, where a flock of Canada geese was nibbling at the water weeds. The streets of Lowell were visible through the trees on the other side of the park.

"Isn't this a beautiful little town?"

Francesca jumped. She'd been lost in thought, confused by C.J.'s come-on, and hadn't seen Marty walking beside her. She looked at him warily.

"Hey, it's okay. I didn't mean to scare you," he said gently. "I'm Marty Klein." He patted her arm to reassure her, but Francesca pulled back. What was it with these guys? Did they think they could touch every girl they came across just because everyone was away from home for the first time?

"Is something wrong?" insisted Marty. "Did C.J. give you a hard time? You looked upset talking to him."

Francesca's head spun with confusion. Marty wasn't trying to put the moves on her after all. He was being understanding. How could he know that C.J. had terrified her? What did he know about her? Francesca felt suddenly exposed and vulnerable. She wanted to run. But where . . . and what good would it do? Sometime, somewhere, she was going to have to stop and face herself.

"No, I'm fine. Just fine," she lied, pulling herself together. "I'm . . . Francesca." His deep blue eyes held hers with an intensity that unnerved her. Maybe that's what made her feel so uncomfortable around him. His intensity. It infused his whole body and reached out to her, wanting . . . but wanting what? She couldn't put her finger on it. But Eve was right. Marty really was kind of weird in a quiet, powerful way. Or maybe mysterious was a better word. . . .

Francesca looked away, deliberately concentrating on the pretty yards they were passing—the big maple trees that would soon be a blaze of reds and yellows and oranges, and the purple and rust-colored chrysanthemums that were providing the final flush of summer to the flower beds.

"It seems to be a very nice place," Francesca finally said. "But I must admit, I've only seen it from the windows of the taxi."

"I wandered around a bit this morning," said Marty. "Before the shops were opened or anything. I had a private viewing, you might say."

Francesca looked at him curiously. Marty was certainly independent. Strange places usually unnerved her.

"I'm kind of looking forward to living in a small community this year," he continued, absorbed in his surroundings.

"Are you from a big city?" Francesca asked politely.

"I guess you'd have to call New York a big city," he replied, smiling at her. "I'm from Brooklyn, right across the river from Manhattan." Francesca swallowed hard. He had the sexiest dimple in the whole world on his right cheek.

"Brooklyn! Isn't that where all the crime is, where people are always getting knifed or mugged or shot?" exclaimed Francesca. "There always seems to be at least one such story on the news every night."

Marty laughed a deep, rumbling laughter. Francesca liked it, but it made her shiver.

"Let's just say I wouldn't believe everything you see on TV about New York," he said. "It gets a bad rap from the press. It's a great place, lots of excitement." Again his blue eyes held hers. "Where's your home?"

"Well, I come from Boston," replied Francesca, feeling another pang of homesickness. Life in the beautiful home on West Haviland Drive was really part of the past now. "But when I was little, we lived on a farm in Vermont."

"So Lowell is no big deal to you, then," remarked Marty. "Don't all Vermont towns look like this?"

Francesca laughed. "Not all, but some are really quaint—just like this one."

Their conversation had carried them to the intersection of Main Street and Lowell Avenue in the very center of town.

"That's the man himself," said Marty knowledgeably, directing Francesca's gaze to a tall bronze statue atop a rustic fieldstone base standing in the middle of the intersection. Yellow marigolds and red geraniums clustered cheerfully around the bottom. "Sam Lowell," he announced. "Founded this town in seventeen twenty-five."

Francesca giggled. "One of the earth-shattering bits of information you learned on your tour this morning."

"But of course," Marty replied. "I checked out everything. Figured I better know a little about my new home."

Francesca looked at him out of the corner of her eye, surprised to discover she'd actually relaxed while they were talking. He was staring at the statue, as if he were trying to see into its very core. Yes, that's it, thought Francesca, admiring the chiseled lines of Marty's face that gave his rough features a subtle sensitivity she hadn't noticed at first. That's what he makes me feel like when he looks at me . . . like he's trying to see inside me, to understand what I'm made up of. She frowned. One thing she didn't want Marty Klein to discover was what she was made up of, what went on inside. It was too dangerous.

"I wonder why there aren't any really old buildings around if Lowell has been here since seventeen twenty-five," she asked, trying to keep the conversation light.

"Elementary, my dear Francesca," said Marty, suddenly launching into a perfect rendition of Sherlock Holmes talking to his sidekick, Watson. The Brooklyn twang was miraculously replaced by an upper-crust English accent. "The Great Fire of eighteen eighty-six did most of them in—sad to say, but true."

Francesca had to laugh. Well, one thing was for sure, she thought with admiration, this guy could be a lot of fun.

Another half a block along and they were outside Tony's. The sign over the door said, in Old English lettering, Famous Since 1982. Lowell even had a classy pizza joint, thought Francesca, silently wondering if pizza could really taste good if it wasn't served in some greasy, neon-flashing dump. While waiting for the rest of the gang to catch up, Francesca looked up and down, trying to orient herself to this new world. The main shopping district was only a couple of blocks long and clustered on the one street. There was a record shop, a couple of shoe stores, and a sports equipment emporium. Right across the street was a neat-looking restaurant, The Proverbial Herb, its front windows filled with herbs growing in pots. It looked funky and fun.

A sign at Lowell Avenue indicated the direction to Lakeside Mall and the beach. From her map, Francesca knew that the beach would be on Long Island Sound, which wasn't like the real beach with its pounding ocean waves she was used to around Boston, but it'd probably still be nice for a picnic on a warm spring or autumn day. In a moment of weakness she allowed herself to imagine a picnic with Marty, the two of them wrapped up in a beach blanket, watching the sea.

"Hey, man, you jiving us about the pizza party?" sang out Clive, dancing past Francesca and up to C.J. "Or were you just seeing how far us group of fools would follow you for the promise of a free slice of the old pepperoni and mushroom?"

"Now, look here," C.J. practically barked. Francesca

jumped. "When C.J. Rollings says he's going to do something, he does it." Francesca stared at him. What was it with this guy? A hard, defensive look etched his face.

"Hey, man, just checking out the action. Didn't mean to offend," came back Clive, his eyes wide with surprise and hurt.

"Well, I said I was paying for it, and I meant it," C.J snapped. He turned to the crowd clustered around the entrance of Tony's. "Okay. Everyone eat as much as you want. C.J. Rollings is feeling generous today."

"What a jerk," whispered Iris as she sauntered by. Francesca silently agreed and followed Marty through the door.

✳ V ✳

"**W**HAT A DISASTER!" GROANED C.J., SLUMPING down on his bed and letting his head fall heavily into his hands. What a complete and total disaster of an evening! And the day had started out so well, too, he thought. He'd woken up feeling good about himself and surprisingly confident about the year ahead. Now he wasn't sure of anything, except that he'd done it again—made an ass of himself . . . like he always seemed to. Okay, so he had been trying to impress Francesca when he first invited everyone down to Tony's. But was that so horrible? She was the best-looking piece of action around this place and he'd wanted her to think he was a big deal. He handled her dumping all over him just fine. No sweat. After all, Serena had certainly provided adequate compensation. For the first time in a long while, walking along with his class-mates, he'd felt like a normal kid, one of the gang.

C.J. clenched his fist and punched his pillow full force. So why had he blown it? Why had he let Clive get to him? Why had he said that stupid thing about being generous?

Hell, if you could just hear yourself sometimes, C.J., he scolded himself. If you'd listen to what you're saying.

You sound just like your father. Anything's possible—friends, positions in society, yeah, even acceptance at SPAR—if you just flash around enough of the old green. Everyone will love you. Well, everyone hadn't loved him, and the bill at Tony's had been astronomical. He could tell by the way his classmates looked at him they thought he was a jerk. They were probably still laughing at him.

"Hi ya, C.J.," Michael called out cheerfully, bouncing through the door. "Thanks a lot for the pizza. That was some kind of good."

C.J. gave him a quick look, then relaxed a little when he saw that his roommate wasn't poking fun at him after all.

"Do you mind if I put up a couple of posters?" asked Michael, wandering around the room checking out possible locations. "I might get confused and think I really am in prison if I don't do something to make this place look like home. Humble is one thing, jailbird bare is another!"

"Yeah, sure . . . go ahead," C.J. agreed. Strange. He hadn't thought about making the room any cozier. It seemed fine. Well, maybe not fine-fine, but it was just like all the other rooms in MacCready—two beds, two dressers, two desks, two sets of bookshelves, a couple of closets and lamps, and stark white walls. Maybe it did look a little bleak, but right now that suited his mood just fine.

He lay back on his bed and watched Michael tack up a poster of Gene Kelly, then another of Rudolf Nureyev. Much as C.J. hated to admit it, the room looked better already. Maybe he'd go over to the mall tomorrow and pick up a poster of Nastassia Kinski. There was a great shot of her wrapped around a huge python. It was intense. He wished she would wrap herself around him.

"Hey . . . uh . . . Michael," began C.J. tentatively.

"Yeah?"

"Do you think maybe we ought to maybe paint this place? It says in the handbook we can if we want. We get

our pick of institution-approved, school-contributed pink,
yellow, blue, or green.''

"Sure. Why not. I vote for pink," said Michael, then
burst out laughing. "Just kidding."

C.J. grinned. "That'd sure get people talking. We ought
to do it just for the fun of it."

"Or paint each wall a different color: four walls, four
colors. The four seasons," suggested Michael, standing
back and admiring his posters. He reached up to straighten
the one of Gene Kelly.

"So what do you think?" He glanced at C.J. "You
going to sign up for the talent contest? I thought I might."

The smile died a quick death on C.J.'s face. His mind
suddenly jerked back to the conversation he'd had with
Serena. She'd asked him the same thing, and stupidly he'd
said, "Sure! Why not!" Only the "why not" had a very
easy answer. Because he was scared. Because he didn't
think he was talented. Because he wanted her to think he
had lots of confidence even though he was a coward.

For a moment C.J. studied Michael's face, wondering if
his roommate was mocking him. It couldn't be. Michael
didn't know how insecure C.J. felt at SPAR . . . or about
having Michael as a roommate. Michael was a singer and
dancer, and Michael was good. No . . . Michael was one
of the best. C.J. had learned from Warren at registration
that Michael was one of the few kids in the program on
full scholarship. SPAR had wanted him so badly they were
willing to foot the bill! Now, that was impressive! C.J.
couldn't shake the feeling that his father had bought him
his place at SPAR. It was just the sort of thing his father
would do. His money had always paved the way. But C.J.
was convinced this time it would catch up with him. He
couldn't fool this bunch. At least not for long, and classes
started tomorrow.

C.J. glanced again at Michael, who was nonchalantly
whistling a tune from *Cabaret* while he adjusted his post-

ers, completely oblivious to the fact that C.J. hadn't answered his question. It was just as well, C.J. thought. He didn't have a reply. Desperately he hoped that Serena would forget their conversation.

"Looks good, huh?" Michael flashed a winning smile at C.J. before he stood back to admire the walls.

C.J. studied his roommate quietly. He had never met anyone with such a straightforward, uncomplicated personality. Nothing seemed to phase this guy. Even the way he dressed—parachute trousers, lime-green tennis shoes, broad-striped socks—was relaxed. C.J. was strictly a tweed and button-down collar man. It was a studied look. Michael's clothes were impulsive and fun, but C.J. knew he'd never have the guts to wear them. If nothing else, his father would disinherit him on the spot.

"I suggest we paint the room blue," C.J. said stiffly.

"Great idea! I'll put in an order for the paint. You're in charge of getting the brushes," said Michael casually, putting the final tack in his posters. "Let's leave these up for now. They make me feel good."

"Fine," agreed C.J. "I like 'em, too."

"Right now, however, I think I'll go cruise the girls' floor. Want to come?" Michael asked.

"Naaa. Let 'em hunger for me," said C.J. with a mischievous grin.

C.J. felt a mixture of relief and disappointment when Michael finally walked out. The room seemed suddenly very empty. But it was easier to be alone, easier not to have to explain himself to anyone. Especially someone like Michael, who seemed to have no need to explain himself to anyone for any reason whatsoever.

"So, did you get all the classes you wanted?" asked Eve, hanging up her crumpled clothes.

"Yes, thank goodness," said Francesca, sinking into a

chair and throwing her big leather tote bag on the table. "I even got that advanced voice class."

"Hey, that's great," Eve responded, picking up her tennis rackets. "Now, where am I going to put my babies?"

"How come you have two of them?" asked Francesca with awe.

"Well," Eve said, "I use this one—it's very tightly strung and can deliver one fast return—when I play against boys. They play a tougher game than most girls, so I have to get tougher. And this one is for regular tournament play. It's my favorite. Makes the sweetest 'pong' you ever heard."

Francesca giggled.

"Do you play?" Eve asked, finally balancing the rackets in the corner of the room by her bed. Francesca couldn't believe how easily the division of the room had gone. They'd settled it in two seconds flat. Eve had wanted the window bed. She'd wanted the one by the wall. Typical, thought Francesca wryly. Eve is so outgoing, so confident. Naturally she'd want the openness of the window. Francesca didn't like to be so close to public view. The corner suited her much better.

"Well, do you . . . play?" repeated Eve, bringing Francesca back down to earth.

"Chess yes, tennis no," she replied.

"That's a shame. I need a doubles partner here."

"Well, count me out," said Francesca. "I'm about as athletic as . . . as the leg of this table."

"Oh, you mean you're more like a jockstrap—better at giving support," quipped Eve. Francesca's face went bright red. She giggled nervously. It shocked her to hear a girl talk like that. She'd been taught to think whatever you like, but only to say what was absolutely appropriate.

"Right." Francesca smiled. "So you play the tournaments and I'll lead the cheering squad."

Laughing, Eve slid out of her skirt and pulled on a pair

of jeans. She looked even smaller and neater in the slick-
fitting pants that couldn't be more than a size three, mused
Francesca enviously. She glanced down at her own endless
legs.

"I could teach you to play," Eve said finally, looking
Francesca straight in the eye.

Francesca absentmindedly twisted her hair into a loose
knot at the back of her neck, and looked at her roommate
with a mixture of surprise and anxiety. Tennis! It had
always seemed so beyond her abilities! But a little voice
inside her cried, "You've never really tried!" Well, was she
willing to try, willing to possibly make a fool of herself?
Francesca opened her mouth to refuse Eve's offer, but
instead heard herself accepting. After all, the voice inside
chided her, this whole year is going to be a series of
challenges. Why not add tennis? Go for it! And maybe
. . . just maybe you can do it!

"Sure. Why not!"

❋ VI ❋

FRANCESCA DROPPED DOWN ON HER BED, SIGHING HEAV-
ily with relief. Her bookbag fell over the edge and hit the
floor with a loud bang. She didn't even jump. It was
Wednesday already! The first week of classes was almost
over! She'd survived! Actually, it hadn't been so bad since
most of the classes were the same ones she'd have been
taking back at Newton High if she'd been there for her
senior year. The real challenge—the acting and singing
and dance classes—began next week. But Francesca didn't
want to think about that now. It just felt good to know that
the whole program was under way and she was handling it
all okay . . . except for Iris.

Francesca sighed again, but out of pure frustration this
time. She'd tried. She'd tried hard to be friendly to Iris—
smiling when they passed each other, inviting her to sit
together at meals—but Iris always gave her a funny look
that made Francesca feel like she'd suddenly lost all her
clothes. Iris always made up some excuse to move on, as
if spending time with Francesca was an unacceptable idea.
Maybe Ellie was right. Maybe Iris was jealous for some

reason. Naw, thought Francesca, unbuttoning her jacket and tossing it over the chair. That was nuts.

Suddenly, a knock sounded at the door. Before Francesca could answer, Iris popped her head around the side. "Frannie?"

For a moment she was startled. Francesca cringed inside, but managed a smile. She hated being called Frannie or Fran. Her name was Francesca. Why did some people have such trouble with that?

"Yes?"

"Can we come in?" Iris asked with a conspiratorial giggle. "We want to talk to you about something."

"Sure," Francesca replied, completely confused by Iris's sudden change of attitude. She'd stared right through her at lunch just two hours ago.

Iris breezed into the room in yet another outfit—the third one of the day—with a girl Francesca didn't know on her heels.

"Oh . . . do you two know each other?" gushed Iris, sliding into her *Better Homes and Gardens* model hostess act.

Francesca and the other girl eyed each other uncomfortably.

"No, we don't," said Francesca.

"Then allow me. Sue Bloom, this is Francesca Minelli. You know, the one who had us all in such a panic before the opening assembly last week. Oh, I tell you, Frannie, we were quite breathless with expectation. We really thought you *were* somebody."

"Sorry," mumbled Francesca, not exactly sure what she was apologizing for. Was Iris really trying to bug her? Iris's clear green eyes and sparkling white smile revealed nothing.

"She *is* somebody," piped up Eve, suddenly flying into the room. She grabbed a sweater from her closet. "But you see, it takes a somebody to know a somebody. This somebody is going to the bookstore." She walked to the door and then suddenly turned around with a smile on her face.

"By the way, Iris," Eve said slowly, obviously enjoying herself, "I noticed you signed up for the talent contest. That was very brave of you. I'm sure we're all impressed. But in case you came here to find out if Francesca here was planning to do the same, don't worry. She's not planning to show you up this time. . . ."

And with that the door closed behind her.

An uncomfortable silence filled the room. Francesca turned to give Iris an apologetic smile, but something in Iris's face stopped her cold. A look of intense fury was dancing across her face, as her eyes focused steadily on Francesca.

"Don't listen to Eve," Francesca mumbled self-consciously. "She just likes to—"

"No, no!" Suddenly the expression on Iris's face softened into a big smile. "Forget it." She waved her arm in a gesture of regal dismissal. "I assure you Sue and I have better things to do than pay attention to that kind of drivel."

Francesca grinned, eager to smooth things over. Iris's quick change of mood seemed a little unreal, but there was no point in pressing the issue. "Well, I'm glad you feel that way," Francesca responded. "Because I certain—"

"Oh," Iris interrupted her, indicating she wanted the subject closed, "speaking of Sue, did you know she's from Tennessee? Can you imagine? I never knew anyone from Tennessee myself, so this is a real experience. And the cutest thing . . . she's a comedienne. Now, isn't that just about the bravest thing you ever heard? You know how hard it is for women to make it in the world of comedy. I keep telling her she should give it up and be a character actor. With her face, she'd be a natural, don't you think?"

Sue smiled adoringly at Iris, but Francesca cringed at

Iris's obvious insensitivity. Sue wasn't beautiful, not by a
long shot. But she had an interesting, open face with
friendly though irregular features, which always seemed to
be in motion, as if she were really half a dozen people
vying for expression. Francesca bet she was good at im-
personations, and would indeed probably make a good
character actor, but Iris had pointed this out in the most
unflattering way possible. She'd made it sound deroga-
tory—or maybe it was just the southern accent. Together
with Iris's busily batting eyelashes, it made everything
sound like some corny line from *Gone With the Wind*.

"Well, now that we all know each other," Iris went on,
seemingly unaware of any pain she might have caused,
"let's get on with the business at hand. Now, Frannie, are
you going to be in the talent show? It's only two weeks
from tonight, you know. Not much time."

"I . . . I don't think so," said Francesca uneasily. "I
didn't work much on my singing over the summer."

"Oh, you're just being shy," gushed Iris, turning to
Sue. "Can you imagine this gorgeous creature actually
being shy? Now, come on, Frannie dear. Admit it. You're
just shy, right?"

Francesca smiled self-consciously. "Yeah . . . I guess
so. I guess I'm just not ready to go up in front of all those
people yet. I'd feel kind of naked. I can't even get used to
people in the hall seeing me in my bathrobe."

Francesca relaxed a bit when her two visitors laughed at
her joke. Maybe Iris had had a change of heart and really
wanted to try to be friends. Francesca was certainly willing
to give it a try. She wasn't used to having enemies, if
that's what she and Iris had been all week. Maybe she'd
just misinterpreted Iris's looks. Her mother was always
telling her she shouldn't be quite so sensitive.

"Well, I've got the perfect solution, then," said Iris
brightly. "In fact, that's why Sue and I are here."

Sue gave Iris a questioning look and opened her mouth to speak, but Iris cut her off.

"I guess we're all a little nervous about getting up the first time," said Iris. "I know I am. Simply terrified. So how about the three of us doing an ensemble act? Sue's all ready to go."

"Wh . . . What . . . !?" stammered Sue.

"I . . . we . . . thought the number out of *A Chorus Line,* 'At the Ballet,' would be appropriate," Iris barreled on, completely ignoring Sue.

"Why don't we go down to the lounge and discuss it," interrupted Francesca. "I'll make us a cup of tea." Basically, she just wanted to get out of her room. Iris made it seem very small and stuffy.

"Grand idea," said Iris, all enthusiasm. "Count on a Boston girl to offer tea. How wonderfully proper."

Francesca led the way down the hall and into the lounge at the end. In one corner was a little kitchenette with a small refrigerator, stove, and sink. Perfect for late-night snacks. Francesca put the tea water on and found some cups in a cupboard.

"Now then, let me tell you all about it," said Iris, moving over on the sofa and patting the seat next to her. Francesca hesitated, then sat down. "It's a cinch. Sue's going to do the 'pretty is what it's all about' bit."

"But, Iris—" tried Sue once again.

"You know, the girl who's all freaked out because she's cute but not pretty," continued Iris, "and has just realized that it's pretty that gets you the job?"

Again Francesca cringed. Surely Sue had felt this obvious barb about her looks.

"I get the sexy role. . . . Lucky me, huh?" Iris giggled loudly. "And I . . . we . . . thought you'd be perfect for the title role, singing about how great going to the ballet used to make you feel." Iris turned her wide, innocent-looking eyes on Francesca. "Sound okay?"

Francesca nodded numbly.

"Great, then Sue and I'll work out a rehearsal schedule and drop it by later," gushed Iris, standing up. "Come on, Sue. We have work to do."

Francesca slumped back on the sofa, trying to collect her thoughts. She felt like she'd just been run over by a truck—a big sixteen-wheeler named Iris Setlow. She'd never even said she'd join Iris's ensemble. She'd just agreed it sounded like a good idea. And it was a good idea. She just wasn't sure if it was smart to get sucked into Iris's ensemble act. Something just didn't seem right. Why hadn't Iris let Sue do some of the talking instead of rudely cutting her off all the time? What had Sue been trying to say?

✳ VII ✳

"**E**XCUSE ME. IS THIS YOUR KETTLE OF WATER?"

Francesca looked up. Ellie was standing beside the steaming kettle. She'd completely forgotten she'd put it on. Iris's constant chatter had really sent her spinning.

"Oh . . . yes, I was making a pot of tea," said Francesca finally. "Would you like a cup?"

"I'd love it," Ellie replied, carrying the steaming kettle over to the coffee table along with two mugs. She joined Francesca on the couch and put her feet up on the table. The furniture in the room was made out of old packing crates and was just perfect for foot-propping.

"Pour away," said Francesca, greatly relieved that Iris was finally gone.

"You know, I don't trust that girl," said Ellie, sipping the warm brew.

"Who?"

"Iris. She almost ran me down outside. You and she been smoking a peace pipe?"

"I'm not sure. But I think I just signed up to do an ensemble act with her for the talent show." Francesca shook her head. "How'd I get sucked into that?"

"By the human whirlpool, Iris Setlow, biggest mouth south of the Mason-Dixon line," laughed Ellie, then sobered. "I tell you. I'd stay as far away from that girl as you can. I just don't trust her."

"I don't know about trusting her or not," admitted Francesca, "but I certainly don't understand her."

"She's my roommate and I don't even begin to understand her. It's going to be an interesting year in room 308," sighed Ellie. "One of us may not survive."

Francesca laughed. She liked Ellie. She was warm and open and honest. "Might be kind of interesting in room 303, too."

Ellie grinned. "I guess what you're saying is we've all been put in with some stranger and are going to have to learn to cope, right?"

"Yeah," agreed Francesca. "One way or another."

"And I used to complain about having to share with my kid sister," quipped Ellie, staring into her cup of tea. "Now those seem like the good old days."

The girls laughed and accidentally sloshed tea all over the table.

"What are you doing at SPAR?" asked Ellie when they'd cleaned up the mess. "I mean, what's your act?"

"I suppose I'm primarily a singer," said Francesca modestly. "But I've done quite a bit of acting since I got to high school. And you?"

"I'm kind of a jack-of-all-trades, master of none, but I prefer acting," replied Ellie, then leaned forward and stage-whispered, "Just don't tell my mother that. She'd like nothing more than for me to be a famous actress. I wouldn't want her to know her plans for me agree with mine! She'd never, ever back off then! She's already planning her outfit for the Academy Awards banquet a couple of years down the road! You cannot believe how pushy she is!"

"Wow, you must be good!" exclaimed Francesca, once again worrying about the top-notch competition at SPAR.

"Not really," said Ellie matter-of-factly. "My mother just wants me to be."

"Is your mother one of those housewives who pushes her kids to be the professional she always dreamed of being but never was?"

"I wish," said Ellie with uncharacteristic bitterness. "Just the opposite. My mother's an actress and fairly successful."

"She is!" said Francesca. "What's her name?"

Ellie looked embarrassed for a moment, then, after taking a deep breath, murmured, "Danielle Harper."

"You mean Danielle Harper of *Newport Lives,* prime-time TV's hottest soap?!"

"You got it."

"And she wants you to follow in her footsteps, right?"

"Another bull's-eye, but she also wants me to go beyond that . . . far beyond. Like I said, she's already got her outfit picked out for the Academy Awards."

"Gosh, Ellie, that sounds like a lot of pressure on you," said Francesca sympathetically. She couldn't believe Ellie's mom was the famous Danielle Harper. Ellie was so low-key, and Danielle Harper was such a big star. Her face was always on the cover of the *National Enquirer.* No wonder Iris made Ellie uncomfortable. She didn't need someone else like Danielle Harper in her life.

"I would appreciate you keeping this piece of news to yourself," said Ellie.

"Of course, Ellie. I can see how you would want to make it on your own here."

"Yeah, I have to find out once and for all if I really have any talent. I don't want just my mother's name opening doors for me."

"You know, I bet you won't be disappointed in yourself," said Francesca encouragingly. "I just have that feeling."

"We'll see; we've got a long year ahead of us," said Ellie tensely, then visibly brightened. "Don't get me wrong, it's not all bad having Danielle Harper for a mother. It sure gives me the chance to meet some real weirdos. I mean, some of her friends are wild like you never imagined wild before."

"How do you mean wild? Like the magazines say—sex, drugs, the works?" asked Francesca.

"I don't know about that. I try to stay out of her private life—I live with my father in New York. But I remember one time I was at this costume party she gave. It was nuts."

"Halloween?" asked Francesca.

"Who knows. Hollywood doesn't need such a logical excuse. But anyway, I went as Lady Godiva—"

"Ellie!" exclaimed Francesca, horrified.

"Oh, don't worry. I went as Lady Godiva after the mayor of whatever town it was she rode through in the raw told her to clean up her act. So I was well dressed. I just thought it was a funny idea to explain to people when they asked who I was."

Francesca giggled.

"But this gorilla kept putting the moves on me. I didn't mind too much. He had a wonderful voice—deep and sexy—and he was tall. So I had great visions of this Paul Newman type under all that polyester fuzz. I even let him talk me into a stroll in the garden. I mean . . . how corny, huh?"

"It sounds wonderfully romantic," sighed Francesca.

"Well, let me tell you how romantic it was," laughed Ellie. "This guy starts to take off his costume—we were by the pool. He's short. I mean, really short—he'd been looking out of two small holes in the neck of the costume.

And about as attractive as an ugly Woody Allen. Can you imagine?''

Francesca was rolling with laughter. Her sides ached and she had trouble catching her breath.

''The plot thickens,'' continued Ellie. ''So I'm trying politely to get back to the party and investigate a good-looking zebra I'd seen, and this guy, half-in, half-out of this gorilla suit, starts attacking me. I mean really going nuts. It felt like he had eight hands, and he was strong for such a wimp. He even ripped my costume. Jerk!''

Francesca stopped laughing. Her mind began to drift. How could Ellie treat it all so lightly? Her mind raced back to the year before. Damian's hands . . . all over her. Had she fought him? Had she begged him to stop? She couldn't remember. She just remembered breathing heavily, wanting him to go and yet stay, too. . . .

Francesca shuddered, willing herself back to the present.

''What did you do?'' she whispered hoarsely.

''I managed to knock him backwards into the pool.'' Ellie laughed. ''Thank God it was the shallow end. That stupid outfit probably weighed two tons wet. He could have drowned.''

''Did you help him out?''

''What for? He didn't deserve my help,'' said Ellie indignantly through her laughter.

Francesca laughed, too . . . but she felt like crying. It was too hard to admit that she couldn't hold her own with boys—that they overwhelmed her too easily. Laughing was easier.

Suddenly Francesca's head began to pound. The stress of pretending to feel one way while another emotion was surging within was taking its toll.

''I've gotta go back to my room and study,'' she murmured to Ellie, quickly standing up. She didn't miss the look of hurt surprise on her new friend's face. Smiling apologetically, Francesca hurried back to the safety of her dorm room. She needed time to think. Alone.

But she wasn't in her room more than a few minutes when a knock sounded on her door.

"Yes . . . come in," she called out, quickly standing up.

A head of dark unruly curls and two bright, intense eyes popped around the corner. Marty Klein. Francesca immediately jumped off her bed and straightened her shirt. She wasn't used to receiving boys in her bedroom, and in fact had been very unsure of the coed dorm arrangements.

"Hello, Francesca, can I have a word with you . . . please?" said Marty.

"Um . . . yes . . . of course," Francesca replied nervously, eyeing his crumpled shirt and faded jeans. How different from C.J. With him, every movement and thread was obviously and carefully thought out long beforehand. He looked like a men's fashion ad. But Marty had his own style—that was for sure—and she liked it. "Why not? Please . . . have a seat?"

"No . . . no thanks. I've got to run, but I was just wondering if you'd like to head down to the city . . . New York, that is . . . this coming weekend and play tourist. I could show you around."

"New York? This weekend?" Francesca felt like an idiot repeating Marty's words, but she also felt cornered. The idea of Marty standing in her bedroom was unnerving.

"Yeah. If you'd like. Take the train down, eat a pizza, watch a few muggings," he said, then added quickly, "Just kidding . . . about the muggings part, I mean. I'd look after you, don't worry about that," he added.

Francesca sat down quickly on the side of her bed, wishing she could find the nerve to open the window. The room was suddenly feeling very stuffy, but she was afraid it would make her anxiety too obvious. She swallowed hard.

"You okay?" asked Marty, his voice thick with concern.

"Yes . . . yes," replied Francesca weakly. She wanted to go to New York with Marty. He had the most wonderful smile. She liked the idea of him looking after her. But she didn't like how her heart was racing. It was a warning. No, it was all too confusing. There was too much happening right now. She didn't trust herself.

"Maybe sometime," she stammered, focusing on the toe of her leather Reeboks. Her hair fell forward around her like a protective shield. "But this weekend's going to be kind of filled up with studying. Thanks anyway."

She couldn't bring herself to look him in the eye. His eyes disarmed her completely. So dark and intense, like some huge mystery. She didn't look up until she heard the door close. Then a tear made its way down her cheek. Angrily she brushed it away. Would she ever escape? Would she ever feel comfortable around boys? What had really happened with Damian? Was the past going to haunt her forever? Another tear followed the first. Then another.

* VIII *

FRIDAY EVENING, THE FIRST WEEK FINALLY OVER, FRANcesca lay on her bed a long time thinking about her strong reaction to Marty's invitation. It had been harmless enough. But then her date with Damian had seemed pretty harmless, too . . . at first. Francesca shook her head trying to dislodge the memory, but it stuck fast. Was she always to be haunted by it? She'd been out on pleasant dates before him. She'd been in control. Things had gone well. Why did this one mess torture her so? Francesca knew the answer. She had been powerfully drawn to Damian, and when her body took over, she'd blundered into a situati͏. she'd never been in before. Her mind slipped back to Boston four months ago—to the weeks before the May Dance. She had felt so excited—so alive!

Francesca had been wanting to go out with Damian all year. He seemed very sophisticated and mature, not to mention absolutely gorgeous. Francesca enjoyed talking with him a lot. In fact, often they ate lunch together, sometimes surrounded by friends, sometimes not. It felt wonderful. Which was unusual.

Francesca always felt as if she were on the fringe of the

popular crowd. They liked her, and she them. But they didn't really seem to understand each other that well. Francesca felt different. She was serious about her music and very involved with her family. Still, somehow whenever she was near Damian, even if it was just joking around, Francesca felt a part of things. Like everyone else. And often she would catch herself staring at his lips, wishing they would touch hers.

Someone down the hall was singing loudly, interrupting her thoughts. Francesca wished whoever it was would stop. Restlessly she plumped up her pillow, and as she lowered her head, the May Dance came into focus.

Francesca had desperately wanted Damian to invite her to the dance, but unlike most of her friends, she couldn't get the nerve to call a boy. Especially one so popular. To her it was still the guy's job to do the phoning. But finally, it seemed almost magically, he called with an invitation to the biggest social event of the year.

By the time they arrived at the dance, she was already floating, and the gym itself only added to the magic. Dominated by a huge, floodlit moon suspended from the middle of the ceiling, the room below was lined with beautiful irises and daisies. It was the perfect spring evening atmosphere. She and Damian found a table to themselves in a far corner and began talking easily with each other. It was all so natural . . . so . . . "right" that she couldn't wait for him to kiss her. He waited until the end of the evening.

They were in his car, in the shadow of the big chestnut tree outside her house. She had ten minutes before she was officially "late." Damian knew what time she had to be in, and so Francesca anticipated a warm kiss, after which he would see her to the door. After all, he'd been the perfect gentleman all evening. So when he slid over and draped his arm around her, Francesca was ready. She wanted this moment to happen very much. She'd dreamed of it often.

But she was totally unprepared for what followed.

His lips were warm, much warmer and more demanding than she'd imagined, sending chills, then fire through her whole body . . . wave after wave of it. Time was running out, but Francesca would not pull away from Damian's arms. She wanted more and more. It was as if her mind had completely lost control, letting her body take over.

But then something new in Damian came alive. His arms suddenly held her too tightly. She couldn't move. "Please," Francesca murmured, unsure of what she really wanted, "let go . . ." But his kisses only grew more insistent, his breath uneven. "Damian," she said louder now, "Stop . . . please . . ." But again, it was as if she'd said nothing. Francesca tried to push him away, but she was no match for Damian. Nor was she completely sure she wanted to be. Even now, she could still hear the sighs. Had they been his or hers? She didn't know. She only knew she had to escape to the safety of her own house, away from Damian's passion. Away from her own powerful urges.

Taking a deep breath, Francesca shoved Damian away with all her might. This time he did not resist. Instead, he glared at her angrily. "So," he muttered, placing both hands on the steering wheel, "You're one of those. . . . You want it, but . . ." He let the end of his thought dangle painfully in mid-air.

For a moment, Francesca froze. Desperately, she wanted to explain. No, she wasn't "one of those." Or at least she didn't want to be. But seconds later she realized she didn't know how to explain. She was too confused, too frightened . . . too different . . .

Francesca reached for the car door, and dashed up the cobblestone path leading to her front door. For a moment she had the crazy thought that he would follow her. Apologize. Gently kiss away her tears. But he didn't. He's a horrible person, she cried out to herself as she opened the front door. An animal! I never want to see him again! It wasn't until Francesca was alone in the quiet comfort of her own room that she realized she was as responsible as he for what had happened. She'd discovered a part of herself she never knew existed. It was dangerous. It had to be hidden away. Francesca had turned to face the wall of her bedroom, and cradled her head in her arms.

Like she was doing now, in her room at SPAR.

How was she ever to know when she really liked a boy or when it was just the intense physical yearning she now knew lay deep within her ready to boil over again? When was she supposed to say no? How far did one go? When was something that felt so right actually very wrong?

Her head was spinning. The safest thing to do was just stay away from boys; don't let things get started so they could get out of hand. It wasn't worth it. She'd never gone out with Damian again, though on several occasions he had tried to talk to her. She'd put him off. She'd signed up for an extra voice class and kept herself very, very busy. Well, that's what had earned her this place at SPAR, so maybe she ought to be a little thankful for the scene with Damian.

Moments later Francesca was asleep.

"Damn that Zed!" shouted Eve, storming through the door of their room.

Francesca jumped, then rubbed her eyes and checked the clock by her bed. She'd slept through dinner. She stared dumbfounded at Eve, who was charging around the room like a bull before the fight.

"I simply can't understand why Zed would do such a thing. Soooooo dumb!"

"Uh . . . wh . . . what?" asked Francesca sleepily,

grabbing the delicate porcelain statue of a ballet dancer from her bedside table before Eve could knock it over.

"I tell you it's nuts to put us together," raged Eve.

"Put who together? You and Zed? Where together?" said Francesca, still trying to shake her brain free of sleep.

"Earth to Francesca . . . Earth to Francesca. Come in, kid. You can do it," shot back Eve.

Francesca laughed. "All right. All right. So I fell asleep. I don't recall any laws in our faithful handbooks against that. Now, would you calm down long enough to tell me what's going on?"

Eve slumped down on Francesca's bed, looking thoroughly dejected. "It's about Marty."

"What about Marty?!" broke in Francesca hurriedly, feeling the blood rush to her face.

"Well, my, my, at least I know how to get your attention now," teased Eve. "What's your interest in Klein?"

"Uh . . . I . . . nothing," stumbled Francesca.

"Your face just always turns bright red at this time of day, huh?" Eve giggled mischievously.

"No . . . I mean . . . he seems like a nice guy." Francesca's insides were twisting in a million knots, and she couldn't even explain to herself why.

"Well, if this is how you react to every 'nice guy,' " quipped Eve, "you've got a long way to go, baby. And if that's how you feel about Klein in particular, which I'm beginning to suspect it is, maybe you could stand in for me next week in Directing 204."

Francesca looked at her uncomprehendingly. "Huh?" she said dumbly.

"The last minute of the last class of the day, Zed put us together on the same project!"

"And you don't like the assignment?" asked Francesca.

Eve shook her head in exasperation. "My faithful roommate, for a smart person, you sure are dumb. In case you haven't noticed, Klein and I don't get on too hot. I mean, like two seconds in the same space is about it. Then we start arguing. You've seen us.''

"He can't be that bad," said Francesca.

"There goes your face again," Eve said. "Anyone ever tell you how cute you are with a bright red face?''

Francesca hurled her pillow at her roommate. Eve ducked and the pillow flopped harmlessly against the wall.

"As a matter of fact, Klein *can* be that bad. And worse! Not personally. But professionally, he and I are worlds apart. Drives me nuts with his puritanical ideas about the 'art' of the theater. So good old Zed puts us together on the same project. 'So we can learn to work with people who have differing views.' I may not survive next week,'' concluded Eve dramatically, pulling out a banjo case from beneath her bed and tuning up.

"A banjo! You play banjo?'' Francesca's eyes widened. Eve was a continual bag of surprises.

"Naaa. I just walk around with it to look cool,'' Eve joked. "Actually, picking away on this old thing is about the best cure I know for a case of chronic frustration, which is exactly what I have right now. Damn Zed!'' She slipped picks on the fingers of her right hand, and in two seconds the room sounded like a recording studio in Nashville in full session.

"That's from *Bonnie and Clyde*, isn't it?'' asked Francesca, awed by her roommate's talent.

"Dern-tootin','' Eve replied, affecting a hillbilly accent. "That's 'Foggy Mountain Breakdown.' ''

"That's neat,'' said Francesca, tapping her foot in time. "Why don't you play it in the talent show?''

"I might.''

Francesca watched Eve's fingers fly over the strings, then added mournfully, "I kind of wish I hadn't signed up with Iris.''

"Good thinking, but too late. That girl is bad medicine, I tell you,'' Eve said, slipping into a blue work shirt and wrapping a red bandanna around her neck. Next she pulled on high-stepping cowboy boots, and twirled around in front of the mirror. "Another ten or fifteen inches in the old boobs and Dolly Parton would have some serious competition here."

Francesca laughed.

"It'll throw old Klein for a loop, don't you think?" She twirled around once again.

"Are you two going out?" asked Francesca in a small voice, wishing she were strong enough not to care.

"Oh my, now it's jealousy, is it?" teased Eve.

"Of course not," snapped Francesca unconvincingly. "I was just interested."

"Then you might be interested to know that Mr. Martin Klein will be showing up on our humble doorstep in about ten minutes time," Eve said. "He and I have got to get to work on our assignment."

"What! Here! Marty!" burbled Francesca, leaping off her bed and grabbing her bookbag in one motion. She had to get out. Out where she could breathe. She was going to choke to death if she stayed in that room one minute longer.

"Hey," said Eve with concern. "Don't freak out. You're welcome to stay."

"No . . . I . . . I . . . couldn't," stammered Francesca, pulling a sweater out of her closet. Quickly she gathered up some history books, and before Eve could stop her, she rushed from the room. Francesca didn't stop running till she was halfway to the library. Then she sank down on an outside bench and gulped in the cool evening air. It was delicious. In a few minutes she stopped shaking and soon got her breath under control.

What in the world am I running from, thought Francesca, slightly horrified at the scene she'd just made. The thought of Marty coming had really flipped her out. But why? Okay, sure . . . he was definitely cute. She remem-

bered the way his dark hair spilled over the open neck of
his shirt, and his lean, strong arms that seemed protective,
not bullish in the least. But it wasn't like she hadn't come
across a few hunks in her life, and no one had made her
lose her cool like that . . . except . . . except . . . Francesca's whole body shuddered. Except . . . Damian.

* IX *

C. J. TOOK A DEEP BREATH AND PUSHED OPEN THE door to the lounge/snack bar in Kenner, called The Pit. It was to be the ''official'' student union for the kids from SPAR. The college kids had another farther up on campus. A rush of talk and laughter engulfed him, drawing him inside despite his hesitation. The word had gone out earlier that everyone was to meet here tonight to celebrate the end of the first week of classes. And by the look of it, he was the last to arrive. The place was hopping with human energy. Sodas and popcorn were disappearing faster than the stars after sunrise, and from the way things looked, the party would be going on at least till then. Everyone seemed to be really up.

Looking at all the smiling faces, C.J. let out a deep sigh. Didn't anyone feel ragged out, like he did? Just from the one acting class, which had only been a lecture, it was easy to see almost everyone had a lot of experience. He hadn't expected it to all be quite so professional. There was no way he could bluff his way through this next year. He was going to have to work his buns off. He was going to have to prove he had talent. C.J. grimaced. Then again, how much talent did he really have? . . .

C.J. turned to leave. He didn't need this scene. He hesitated, hand on the door. So, what was he going to do? Sit in his room while everyone was hanging out down here? That sounded like a lot of fun. Whooop-dee-do! Naw, might as well stay, he thought. Who knows, I might luck out and actually meet a human being in this zoo.

"Hi ya, C.J.," called out Michael, throwing his arm around C.J.'s shoulders and dragging him over to the counter. "Let me buy you a drink. Pepsi or Coke?"

"Uh . . . Coke would be fine. Thanks," mumbled C.J., still unsure if he should leave or stay.

"So tell me," continued Michael, handing him the overfilled glass of Coke. "Are you going to go for the talent show?"

There was that question again. C.J.'s insides churned. He knew he'd told Serena he was planning to sign up, but he figured he'd find some way out of it before he actually had to commit himself. He wasn't ready for that yet.

"Ah, I'll probably give it a miss," bluffed C.J. "My Hamlet's a bit rusty."

"Hamlet! Whoa there. That's pretty heavy stuff; you must be some kind of good."

"Yeah . . . well . . . I guess that was just the best thing I ever did . . . in high school. It went okay."

"Wow, Hamlet with a Texas accent. That must be wild."

"I'm not stuck with this accent all the time," said C.J. defensively. "After all, I am an actor."

"Hey, buddy, no offense meant," said Michael lightly.

"I saw you dancing the other day," said C.J., trying to get the conversation on a different tack. "When I came by the practice rooms. You looked pretty good. How long have you been dancing seriously?"

"Since never," Michael replied, looking slightly embarrassed.

"I don't understand."

"There's not much to understand. My body seems to be able to dance whether I take it seriously or not. I've never seen the point in taking it too seriously."

"You mean, you don't know if you're going to be a professional dancer after all this?" asked C.J. incredulously. If he didn't make it as an actor or singer—if he failed this year at SPAR—he didn't know what he would do. He was counting on it. He'd thrown all his eggs into one basket, which is exactly what his father was always telling him not to do . . . and probably why he always did it anyway. For the first time, C.J. wondered if maybe his dad was right after all.

"Not really," said Michael, rocking his chair on its two back legs. His powerful thighs strained against his tight jeans. "I might, of course. Dance is one of my options; that's how I see it. But I'd just as soon be writing or playing baseball or lying on some hot beach with Priscilla." Michael threw back his head and laughed with abandon as if life was nothing but a joyful experience.

"Who's Priscilla?" queried C.J., trying to make polite conversation as he allowed his eye to travel around the room. Suddenly he spotted Serena a few tables over. It occurred to him that what he really needed was a little heavy action with her, to forget all his self-doubts for a while.

"My girl," replied Michael, adding forlornly, "back in Chicago."

"Nice name," said C.J. absentmindedly. "But if I were you, I'd stick with dance."

"Yeah? Well . . . thanks," stammered Michael, his face red with embarrassment. "You really think it looked okay?"

"Sure." C.J. nodded quickly. He was afraid Serena

would leave before he made his move. "Well, I think I'm going to circulate, get to know some of my classmates," he said quickly. "And one in particular."

Michael followed C.J.'s line of vision to Serena. "Well, my man, you've got good taste. I was going after that one myself. But please . . . be my guest."

Serena was wearing a pair of form-fitting stirrup pants over a dance leotard. Her perfectly proportioned torso was shrink-wrapped in midnight-blue Lycra, making a dramatic backdrop for her tangle of golden hair. Her eyes were heavily made-up and sparkled mischievously as she related some story to the others at her table. C.J. was too far away to catch what was being said, and too busy working out a plan to get her off on her own to care. He didn't feel like being part of the team right now. He'd been around these people enough for one week.

C.J. ducked quickly into the bathroom to comb his hair. When he came out, he almost tripped over Serena. She smiled up at him.

"Would you . . . ?" began Serena.

"What do you say we . . . ? said C.J. simultaneously, having trouble tearing his eyes away from the plunging neckline of Serena's leotard.

"I'm sorry . . . go ahead," giggled Serena.

"No, I interrupted you," replied C.J. gallantly.

"Well, I couldn't help noticing that you were getting a little bored with the scene here," said Serena with a forced casualness. "Would you like to go somewhere else . . . somewhere where we can talk about something besides theater for a while?"

C.J. laughed with relief. "That's exactly what I was thinking. If I see one more dancer flex his muscles, or hear one more singer climb the scale—"

"Or one more actor doing a Brando imitation," laughed Serena, her large blue eyes dancing with abandon from beneath her blond mop.

C.J. laughed even harder. It felt good to laugh. Really laugh way down in your gut until the muscles hurt. Yes, indeed, this blond bombshell was going to be the perfect antidote to his depression. He could tell already that she liked him.

"It's such a beautiful night, why don't we walk to town and see what kind of action old Lowell can throw at us," suggested C.J., putting his arm around her shoulder and leading her out the door.

Serena giggled. "Sounds like a good plan to me."

As the heavy lounge doors swung shut behind them, the din of the party was replaced by a full chorus of tree frogs and crickets.

"Wow, it's so noisy in the country," Serena remarked, shivering slightly in the autumn chill.

"Here, take my jacket," said C.J., swinging it quickly around her shoulders. Much as he hated to cover up her luscious body, he had to admit she looked pretty cute in his huge tweed jacket. Besides, it would give him the pleasure of taking it off her later. . . .

"What are all those bugs?" continued Serena, unaware of C.J.'s lingering eyes.

"Don't know," he said. "I come from Dallas. To me, bugs mean it's time to call the exterminator."

Serena laughed. "Well, nighttime noises in L.A. are someone yelling at a neighbor's dog to shut up, except they don't usually use such polite language."

They laughed together, then walked along in silence for a while listening to the strange new noises of their exciting new home. C.J.'s hand rested casually on Serena's shoulder. Her hair cascaded down and gently tickled his arm. He toyed with the soft, silky strands, and slowly he began to relax. The knot in his stomach began to unwind. He was on familiar territory now. He'd proven himself on this stage enough times to feel real confidence. Even his father didn't seem such a threat at times like this.

"Oh, what a cute little café," said Serena enthusiastically when they reached The Proverbial Herb.

"Want to check it out?" said C.J.

"Sure . . . why not," Serena agreed.

C.J. held open the door for her. The smell of freshly baked bread wafted out.

"It's pretty crowded," observed Serena. There were only half a dozen or so tables and all of them were occupied by college kids.

"Yeah . . . well, maybe we could just order something take-out and sit in the park," suggested C.J., thinking he'd come up with the perfect, innocent-sounding excuse to get Serena off alone.

"Great idea! Let's see what they have."

Serena ordered a cup of hot chocolate and a bean sprout and avocado sandwich. C.J. got a ham and Swiss cheese on pita bread, although he wasn't at all hungry, at least not for ham and Swiss. Serena made him feel great. She made him feel like he was in control again, something he hadn't really felt since arriving in Lowell, and he wanted to express his appreciation in the only way he knew how. He grinned to himself and squared his shoulders.

As Serena and C.J. wandered into the park, a soft September breeze was blowing the falling leaves all around them. The night air was crisp and invigorating. C.J. wished he could just run around with abandon, kicking at leaves, swinging on limbs, giving himself up to this wonderful night. But he didn't want Serena to think he was a total jerk. Right now she seemed to think he was pretty neat, and that's the way he wanted to keep it. They found a bench beside the lake. Paddleboats and rowboats were chained up on the shore nearby, and a full moon was making its way over the tops of the trees.

"Oh, doesn't it smell divine?" sighed Serena, sinking down on the bench. "Just divine."

"Mmmmmm," said C.J., sliding down beside her and nuzzling her neck. "But not nearly as wonderful as you."

C.J. almost toppled over as Serena slid away from him.

"Let's see," she said with a nervous giggle. "You had the coffee, right? Here." She handed him the Styrofoam cup. "And I've got the hot chocolate." She giggled again. "I could drink a gallon of this stuff. Kind of makes me feel all warm and snuggly, like sitting in front of a fire on a cold night."

Serena's chatter bombarded C.J., confusing him. So far he'd just gotten good vibes from her, like she really liked him. So, what was happening now? He sure never thought he'd have trouble getting physical with this one. She looked like she would enjoy it as much as he would. So, what was going on? He moved over slightly so he wasn't quite pressed against her and accepted the cup of coffee. Maybe she was just playing hard to get. Okay. No problem. He'd faced that situation before . . . and won.

"This sandwich is delish," continued Serena. "Oh, I'm sorry. I forgot to give you yours." She handed him the second sandwich and went on eating, watching the moonbeams dance a lively pas de deux with the waves on the lake.

"Aren't we lucky?" she finally sighed.

"Yeah," agreed C.J. "What a perfect evening, huh? The temperature, the setting, you and me here together." He tried to pull her in close for a kiss. His big move. But again she pulled away—not violently, but gently and insistently. Again, he sat back in confusion.

"No, I mean to be here at Lowell College at all," she continued. "You know how many kids tried out for spots at SPAR."

"Hundreds, I guess," said C.J. disinterestedly.

"Thousands. That's what I heard. Thousands," whispered Serena in awe. "I never thought I'd get accepted. Did you?"

"Uh . . . no . . . well, maybe. I didn't think about it too much."

"You mean, you just figured you'd make it?" asked Serena in disbelief.

C.J. shifted nervously. How could he explain to Serena that even if he were the worst actor in the world, his father's money could have bought him a position at SPAR? No one ever refused Bull Rollings when he whipped out the old checkbook. C.J. wondered again if his talent or his father had gotten him to SPAR.

"Well, I'm so proud to be part of all this, I could bust," announced Serena, finishing off her sandwich. "I just hope I can live up to SPAR's expectations of me. I mean, what if I'm not really as good as they think I am? There are a lot of talented kids out there who'd love to have my place, I'm sure—but then, I guess I have to have some talents if they accepted me, right?"

C.J. tried to take a deep breath, but it felt like someone was choking him. His heart pounded. What was going to happen to him when classes started tomorrow? Would everyone see he had no talent? Did everyone guess his father probably bought him the spot at SPAR? C.J.'s stomach lurched. SPAR might be the beginning of great things for most of these kids like Serena, but it could be the end for him.

"By the way." Serena studied his face excitedly. "I checked the sign-up sheet for the talent contest. You haven't signed yet. How come? I can't wait to hear you sing. I'm sure you're wonderful!"

C.J. was afraid to speak. How could he tell her he didn't have the nerve to sign up?

"Uh . . . we ought to be getting back, I think," C.J. finally stammered, suddenly jumping to his feet.

"Oh, no," said Serena, her big blue eyes staring sadly up at him. "I was having such a nice time. Let's not go yet. Is it because of the contest? Should I shut up about it?''

Looking down at her beautiful face, C.J. almost told her the truth, but his ego was in too much trouble now. That familiar feeling of worthlessness had washed over him. He felt empty and useless.

''No, no! That's not it. I'm signing up. But it's been a long week. I just think we ought to go,'' he said gruffly, turning away so he didn't have to deal with the pain and confusion on Serena's face.

He had enough of his own.

✳ X ✳

"OKAY, KID, UP AND AT 'EM," SHOUTED EVE ENthusiastically, yanking back the covers on Francesca's bed. Francesca cringed, hiding her eyes as the early morning light poured into the room. With a struggle, she blinked away the final vestiges of sleep and focused on her roommate. Eve was dressed and scrubbed and ready to go. Francesca groaned and rolled over, trying to bury her head under the pillow.

"Hey, you can't go back to sleep," demanded Eve, rocking the bed. "This is the first day of the real thing. Remember? Time to prove if you have 'the right stuff.' "

"One more cliché and I'll be too sick to go to class," protested Francesca, trying to wrest the covers back from Eve. How could her roommate be so excited about the SPAR classes starting today? Was she so sure about having the right stuff? "Anyway, it's only seven. Classes don't start till eight."

"Yeah, but don't you want breakfast?"

Breakfast! Francesca's stomach heaved at the thought. It was too early for breakfast. Besides, how could anyone think of food at a time like this? Francesca had hardly slept all night thinking about the classes starting today.

"Well, this kid is hungry enough to eat Cream of Wheat," Eve said, making a face, "and I want you to know I can't stand the stuff."

Francesca's giggles were muffled by the blanket she'd managed to steal back and pull up to her forehead.

"You get one final chance to accompany Eve Jacobson, soon to be one of the world's great directors, to breakfast," said Eve with a dramatic flourish, sweeping her cotton turquoise quilted jacket around her shoulders and heading for the door. "One day, when you're writing an article on me for the *National Enquirer*—you know, one of those 'I knew her when' type deals—you'll be able to say it was Cream of Wheat that was accountable for Ms. Jacobson's meteoric rise to fame, that you were there when I downed two bowls."

Francesca giggled and tossed her pillow at Eve.

"Ah . . . you have no appreciation for the great," said Eve melodramatically.

"Send me a postcard from the top," joked Francesca. "And when *you* write an article on me, you can say with all honesty that it was Ms. Minelli's impossible roommate who derailed what could have been one of the great voice careers of all times, because singers need sleep. Get it? Sleep . . . you know, when you close your eyes and breathe slowly and have wonderful dreams."

"Oh . . . right," deadpanned Eve. "Okay, you sleep and I'll just slip quietly into this magnificent day and get a head start on things. I can just taste that coffee now." Eve closed her eyes and breathed deeply.

"All right. All right. You've finally done it," said Francesca with mock distress.

"I'll save you a seat in the cafeteria," Eve offered, one hand on the doorknob. "How's that?"

"It's a deal." Francesca leaped out of bed as the door

closed with a bang behind Eve. In an effort to ward off her jitters, Francesca snapped on the radio and wiggled the knob until she found a classical station. Beethoven filled the room and washed over Francesca, assuring her that the world still held great and wonderful things. Her confidence began to return. This year at SPAR would give her the chance to play Beethoven, to sing Sondheim, to act in some of the world's great classics of the stage . . . which reminded her of last night. Her heart sank at the thought. She'd had the first rehearsal with Iris and Sue for their talent show act. It was weird. Iris had been so excited about the whole idea in the beginning, but she'd hardly known her lines last night, and Sue was even worse. They had stumbled through rehearsal like they'd never seen the music or words before! What was going on? Well, maybe they'd all get it together at the next rehearsal. She hoped so. She had to admit she was getting kind of excited about the whole idea, especially since her voice had sounded so much better last night than she'd expected after her summer of leisure. Plus, to do the show right off the bang like that would really help her over her jitters.

Francesca shivered with a mixture of anticipation and dread, and threw open her closet. Now . . . what to wear.

The first thing she pulled from her closet was a pair of red stirrup pants. She'd bought them on a whim the day before leaving for Lowell. Pop fashion had never been her scene—her parents discouraged it, telling her that something like a classic tweed jacket would never go out of style, so why waste money on something that would be useless next year . . . like the red stirrup pants. But the idea of leaving home had made her feel independent and impulsive, so she'd bought the pants anyway. Now she wasn't so sure she would ever wear them. They were kind of tight. Well, maybe not tight as in too small, but they didn't leave much of her figure to the imagination. Maybe

she should have bought them in black instead. Black was a
little less conspicuous.

Next she brought out gray flannel trousers. Nice, classic
gray flannel trousers, but they looked so boring. She remembered how some of the other kids were dressed yesterday: Michael in his neon-green parachute trousers, Ellie in
her funky overalls, even Marty in his faded jeans. Her
mind lingered awhile on the image of Marty leaning against
the doorjamb of her room, trying to talk her into going to
New York with him, saying he would look after her. Goose
bumps rose slowly over her whole body. She smiled. For a
moment she imagined his mouth on hers, and a sigh
escaped her lips. Abruptly she pushed the thought away
and replaced the flannel trousers. Neither held the answers
to her problems.

Suddenly Francesca had an idea. Why not check out
what everyone else was wearing? She rushed to the window and stood for a while watching her classmates wander
down the hill to the cafeteria. Basically, it was a sea of
blue denim. Everyone seemed to have on jeans, even Iris,
who was just emerging from the dorm onto the sidewalk
right below Francesca's window. But her jeans were brand
spanking new, very snug, and beautifully ironed. And instead of the loose, brightly colored tops most of the kids
were wearing, Iris had on a tight turtleneck sweater that
seemed melded to her body. Swinging from her shoulder
was an expensive-looking, oversize leather handbag. Everyone else had knapsacks. Iris was one of those people
who tried so hard to be with-it but never quite made it,
thought Francesca, feeling momentarily sorry for Iris as
she eyed the southern belle's low-heeled pumps that stood
out in glaring contrast to everyone else's scuffed-up sneakers.
Iris would never look hip, and she sure didn't look like she
was off to schlepp around dirty stages all day. Francesca
frowned. Often she wasn't sure she looked hip, either. She

tried, but sometimes she felt like an actress playing a role
. . . and not very successfully.

Oh my gosh, thought Francesca, checking her watch and
hurrying back to her closet. Eve's going to think I went
back to sleep! Francesca threw on a pair of jeans and
quickly tucked in a bright red flannel shirt. Her favorite.
She'd had it for a couple of years and it was so soft and
cuddly now. Just right for helping her through a nerve-
racking day. Quickly she tossed her notepad, class schedule, and pens into her shocking-orange nylon knapsack and
rushed out the door. It had been her brother's. Carrying it
made her feel closer to the safety of home.

The cafeteria the SPAR students shared with the college
kids was packed, and everyone seemed to be talking at
once at the top of their lungs. Francesca smiled. It was
kind of a nice feeling to mix with the older kids. Most of
them were quite friendly. With breakfast tray in hand,
Francesca scanned the crowds looking for her roommate.
When she finally spotted her on the far side of the room,
Francesca's blood ran cold. Eve was deep in conversation
with Marty Klein! Quickly she looked away. After the
episode in her room last week, he probably thought she
was the rudest person in the world. Well, if he did, maybe
he'd leave her alone, Francesca thought as she kept her
eyes averted. Then she'd be fine. Somehow Francesca
expected that thought to be a comfort. But it wasn't. She
felt sad instead. She didn't really want him to leave her
alone. She just wanted him to be a little less intense . . .
back off a bit.

Francesca watched Marty talking animatedly with Eve,
his blue eyes flashing, his dark curls still tangled from
sleep. He was so cute . . . but so dangerous. Francesca
began looking around for another seat. Spotting Jyl, a
college freshman she'd met outside of her English class,
Francesca was about to walk over when Eve saw her and

motioned her to join them. There was nothing she could do but go.

"Hello, Francesca," said Marty, his smile so warm and embracing that Francesca's pulse raced. She forced herself to look him in the eye and smile back.

"Geez, I thought you'd gone back to sleep," said Eve, spooning up her Cream of Wheat.

"No, I . . ." Francesca was about to say she just had trouble deciding what to wear, but that sounded so dumb. She didn't want Marty to think she was one of those shallow airheads who was only concerned about her wardrobe and makeup. But why should she care what Marty thought about her anyway? "No, I just don't believe in rushing around in the morning," said Francesca.

"Me, either," said Marty. "Mornings should be slow and thoughtful; give you time to get a handle on the day."

Francesca looked at him with surprise. He knew exactly what she meant. Marty's voice was so deep and rich . . . and slow and thoughtful . . . and intense. It seemed to come from all directions and surround her, like she was in an echo chamber. Francesca sat down, concentrating hard on her plate of scrambled eggs.

"Hey, did you read on the bulletin board that free movies will be shown once a week starting this Saturday in Thompson Theater?" said Eve.

"No," replied Francesca, thankful that a light conversation had started.

"Yeah. *Flamingo Kid* this Saturday."

"I haven't seen it," said Francesca. "Is it good?"

"It's lousy," Marty broke in. "A waste of time."

"Lousy! I thought it was wonderful," enthused Eve. "A real statement on the times."

"If you're interested in prehistory," shot back Marty.

"Prehistory!" Eve's voice rose defensively. Francesca looked around nervously. Some of the kids were starting to stare at them. "The summer of nineteen sixty-three was a real bridge between two distinct eras of American history. I thought they did a super job of putting it across in that film."

"Did we see the same movie?" asked Marty.

"Matt Dillon, Richard Crenna, Hector Elizondo?" said Eve, rattling off the names of the lead actors.

"Yep, that's the one," said Marty calmly. "I just don't remember the movie making any sort of impressive statement."

"Well, it was subtle," replied Eve indignantly. "That was the beauty of it. They used a normal kid from an everyday family to illustrate the relative simplicity of a teenager's life in America before the madness of the later sixties—the Vietnam War, drugs, Kennedy's assassination."

"With your imagination, you should be writing for the movies," snapped Marty. "*Flamingo Kid* was a two-bit sitcom about some jerk who made a lot of money without a college education, which impressed our young hero, Matt Dillon, into deciding not to go to Columbia after all, until he learned that his hero made his money ripping people off—cheating. In the end, kid returns to humble home, repentant, realizing his self-made, hardworking father was right after all. Ah . . . what a bunch of schmaltz."

"Now, wait a minute—" began Eve, her eyes shooting sparks.

Francesca laughed lightly, trying to divert their attention. "What happened to the truce you called yesterday?"

Marty looked sheepishly at Eve, who immediately glanced down at her plate, her cheeks burning.

"Well, you know Eve's philosophy," said Marty jokingly.

Francesca gave him a quizzical look.

" 'An argument a day keeps the doctor away.' " He laughed.

"You were arguing as much as she was," Francesca replied, surprised at her own bravado.

"No," teased Marty. "I was discussing, she was arguing."

"Oh, you're going to drive me crazy," retorted Eve, trying to force the smile off her lips.

"You mean—crazier," shot back Marty, and they all cracked up.

Once again retreating into her shell, Francesca studied Marty and Eve. If only she could have a relationship like that with him. Just fun—arguing about movies, laughing at how dumb you sounded. A real friendship. But Marty seemed to get all heavy and serious around her. Or was it the other way around?

"Why, hello, gorgeous!"

Francesca looked up and straight into Iris's eyes. They seemed to glow with an unnatural brightness. Sue was standing two paces behind her, as usual.

"I just wanted to say that you really held the whole rehearsal together last night," gushed Iris while Francesca's face turned scarlet. "No, I mean it. Your voice is sensational. Really fabulous. I think our act is going to open a few eyes around this place." Iris burst into laughter. Sue giggled halfheartedly, but Francesca thought she read more pain than pleasure on her face.

"Well, gotta run, Toots," said Iris through her laughter. "See you at rehearsal Thursday."

"You doing an act with that witch?" asked Marty when Iris had disappeared into the crowd.

"Yes . . . yes . . . an ensemble number for the talent show," murmured Francesca, still confused about Iris's behavior. What had been so darned funny? And why did she say they were going to "open a few eyes"? Their act was going to be the worst one of the whole show if Iris and Sue didn't get it together and learn their parts.

"Well, I tell you, I wouldn't trust that girl as far as I could throw her; and for that matter, I wouldn't even want to get near enough to throw her," said Marty. "Gives me the creeps."

"Oh, she's not so bad," said Francesca, wondering in the same breath why she was defending Iris. "She seems to be pretty excited about SPAR and doing a good job. Can't fault her for that."

"That's about the only thing I couldn't fault her on, assuming her enthusiasm is genuine," came back Marty.

"Okay, my trusty classmates," said Eve, glancing at the huge clock on the wall. "It's ten to eight. Our big debut at SPAR is about to begin. Are you ready?"

"Let's go," said Marty, standing up and taking Francesca's tray for her.

"Onward," chimed in Francesca, picking up on their light mood. And she was excited. Her first class was advanced voice. The perfect start. She might have a lot of other problems to overcome in this world, but one thing she was certain of—her ability to sing. She couldn't wait to get to class, and swung confidently out the door, joining the flow of kids headed for the Kenner Performing Arts Center.

* XI *

C. J. MOVED TOWARD KENNER WITH THE REST OF HIS classmates, trying to maintain a jaunty air, trying to keep his breakfast down. Why, oh why had he let Michael talk him into eggs and bacon? His stomach was going nuts, not to mention his nervous system. In ten minutes his acting class started. In ten minutes the test to see if he had what it took to be an actor would seriously begin. Why did he have the feeling he was walking to the gallows, or about to lay his head down for the guillotine? His acting résumé probably looked as good as anyone's here. Yeah, he'd done a lot of standard stuff like musicals and comedies, but he'd also done Shakespeare. Quite a bit of it. Hamlet was his favorite role of all time, and he'd gotten pretty good reviews doing it. Damn good reviews, if you could trust your local newspaper, which depended heavily on advertising revenue from your old man's oil company!

C.J. shuddered. He wondered how much his father had paid for his spot with SPAR. Sure, he might be two thousand miles away from his father, but in reality his father was still there, beside him, clearing the paths with whatever it took—usually money—so his precious son wouldn't stumble. Well, maybe I'd like to stumble, thought C.J. angrily. Maybe I'd like to stumble so I could pick myself up and stand on my own two feet again. But not here—don't let me stumble at SPAR. Please, oh please let me get through this acting class without disgracing myself.

"Hi, C.J.," said Serena, stepping in beside him and smiling sweetly up at him. "Are you nervous?"

"Hi ya, kid," C.J. replied coolly, hardly glancing down at her. He didn't trust himself with any other emotions today. It was all he could do just keeping his head together about this acting class. "Nervous?! *Moi?* Us Texans have nerves of steel. Didn't you know that?"

Serena giggled. "Then I wish I were from Texas. I feel like a million butterflies just came out of their cocoons at the same time in my stomach. Whew! If I make it through this day . . ."

"Ahhhh . . . don't worry about it, kid. You'll do fine," bluffed C.J. He almost asked her to meet him for dinner later, but his bravado had run out. He might be a basket case by six o'clock. But boy oh boy, would he ever like another chance at Sexy Serena. Last Friday night was just bad timing. A lot of girls liked to act prudish on the first date. Then, by date number two, they've done their "good girl" bit, and are ready for a little action.

C.J. sighed. If only he had the same confidence with acting that he had with girls. . . .

People jostled each other going through the big doors of Kenner. There were nervous apologies and anxious giggles as everyone raced around looking for the right room numbers for their first classes. C.J. headed up the stairs.

"Well, break a leg, C.J.," said Serena, turning down the hall. "My class seems to be on this floor."

"Sure, kid. You, too," said C.J. He wished he and Serena could have just escaped for the day. Rented one of those boats on the lake and found a private cove. She believed in him. He could feel it. And it would be nice to be lost in that for a while. He watched her luscious form work its way through the crowds and his body tingled all over in response.

"Oh, C.J.," shouted Serena, suddenly turning back. "I signed you up for the talent show. Not many spots left and I knew how much you wanted to be in it. Hope you don't mind." She searched his face for approval.

Somehow C.J. managed to smile, and moments later she was gone.

Mind! gasped C.J., holding onto the stair rail for support. It wasn't a question of "mind," it was a question of "couldn't do." He wouldn't be able to get up in front of those kids in just two weeks, probably not even two years! Maybe never! It was as simple as that.

The bell sounded, jerking C.J. out of his nightmare. He ran up the steps and into class.

Everyone was already sitting in a circle. Joan Lincoln, the acting teacher, waited for him to take a seat and then called out their names. His year at SPAR had really started.

There were fifteen or so other kids in the class, and not one of them looked nervous. Not one. Maybe they'd already started acting, thought C.J., wondering if his cool facade was as effective as theirs.

"Okay, everyone stand up and make a tight circle," said Joan, putting away her attendance sheet. "We're going to start off with a relaxation exercise so we all feel a little more comfortable with each other. This first one's called a trust circle. Maybe some of you have done it before."

C.J. almost groaned out loud. He hated these things. Acting was getting up on the stage and playing a role. That was easy. He could relate when he was acting. But getting cozy with his classmates through relaxation exercises just made him tense. He shuffled forward reluctantly and joined hands with the others to form the circle.

"Great. Tighten it up a bit," directed Joan. "Move in as close to each other as possible."

C.J. felt the others press in close around him.

"Now, Chris," said Joan, pointing to a small blond boy, "you stand in the middle of the circle and close your eyes. The object of this exercise is to get you to trust your classmates, because when you get up on stage, you've got to be able to trust them emotionally and physically in order to take the risk of throwing yourself totally into the role you're playing. Got it?"

Everyone nodded.

"Now, Chris, I want you to fall back against the circle," Joan continued. "No, keep your eyes closed. That's all part of building trust. Fall back and the rest of you catch him against your bodies and pass him around by gently shoving him on to the next person. Chris has got to know you're going to be there for him. If you don't let him down in class, he'll start to believe you won't let him down on the stage, and this is essential for good acting. Okay . . . start."

At first Chris fell back stiffly, but as the circle continued to catch him, C.J. could see him relax and start falling back without reservation. But when he fell against C.J., he shifted his pattern, throwing his weight way to the left instead of the right, and C.J., caught by surprise, was unable to support him. Chris started to fall. The guy next to C.J. thrust his body in front to catch him, but Chris was visibly shaken. Joan gave C.J. a sharp look, and he felt his face redden. His first failure.

They did several more exercises, but C.J. didn't feel any more relaxed than when he first walked in.

"Okay, class," said Joan, moving into the middle of the circle, "now we're ready to try a little acting. How about an expression exercise, okay? Everyone take a seat."

A chorus of "okays" that came out like a huge sigh was her response. Acting class was in session.

"I'm sure I don't have to tell any of you," she began, "that often it's not what you say, but how you say it that makes people really get your meaning."

Everyone nodded.

"For instance," Joan continued, "take the words 'I love you.' Wonderful words, right? Very romantic . . . but . . ." She paused for effect. "Suppose I did this. . . ."

Suddenly Joan began clapping her hands and jumping up and down like a little girl. "I LOVE YOU!" she screeched at no one in particular.

The class began to crack up, and C.J. felt his shoulder muscles relax. This teacher was a gas. Maybe he'd survive the year after all.

Joan stopped as suddenly as she'd started and began talking again, motioning for the students to be quiet. " 'I love you' didn't sound so romantic then, did it? I could have been saying anything, simply choosing to use those words to convey the message. For instance, I might have been a three-year-old trying to say thank you for a terrific present." She looked around the class from one to the other. C.J. squirmed uneasily. "Get the picture?"

All the kids nodded solemnly, though a few giggles could still be heard.

"Okay. Now Julian," said Joan, suddenly pointing a finger at a boy with large, sensitive eyes. "You first. Stand in the middle of the circle."

"And you, Gina," continued Joan, pointing to a petite blond girl. "Let Julian play to you. Come on up."

C.J. watched the two move self-consciously into the middle of the room, hardly looking at each other. He was so thankful that he hadn't been called up that he leaned back in his chair and watched with interest.

"Okay, Julian," said Joan. "Let's do hate. I want you to say 'I hate you' to Gina with three entirely different emotions. Say it so we know you mean it, say it so we know you're unsure, and say it so we know you love Gina more than anything. Don't tell us which way you're going to try it first. We'll guess afterwards. It may be helpful to visualize a situation. Just don't verbalize it.''

Julian nodded, turned to Gina, stood deep in thought for a few minutes, and then began.

Suddenly C.J. brought his chair down on all four legs. This guy was good. He had overcome his self-conciousness and done exactly what Joan told him. He was terrific. Each emotion was perfectly clear. Joan called the next couple up. The guy wasn't as good as Julian, but he wasn't bad. Not bad at all. By the time Joan called the third couple up, C.J. realized with horror that she meant to go around the whole room.

"Hey, I'm pretty impressed with you guys," said Joan, smiling broadly after the fourth couple sat down. "You're good. You're going to make my year too easy if you keep this up. Now then . . . let's try another emotion . . . something a little more difficult.''

She put her hands on her slender hips and surveyed the class. "C.J.," she said finally. "How about giving it a try? . . . And Emma. Come on up.''

C.J. felt his pulse go wild, but somehow he got to the center of the room and smiled at the dramatic-looking brunette who was his partner.

"All right," said Joan, hesitating a moment. "Let's do 'I love you.' Love is harder to convey than hate, I think, because it has more subtleties. But you all seem to be up to the challenge. Remember, you can use a situation. Just don't tell us about it.''

C.J.'s ears were buzzing and his knees were threatening to buckle and dump him unceremoniously on the floor. ''I love you.'' Of all the people to pick to say those words, I have to be the worst choice, he thought, desperately praying that the building would catch on fire in the next thirty seconds, or the town of Lowell would be hit by a minor earthquake. Anything to get him out of this assignment.

I've said many things to many girls in my time, C.J.
thought, but "I love you" is not one of them. No way.

"Okay, C.J.," continued Joan. "Try saying 'I love
you' to Emma with anger, joy, and . . . well . . . how
about insincerity? Try saying 'I love you' so it's clear to
the rest of us you don't mean it. Got that?"

C.J. nodded weakly as Joan moved out of the circle and
turned to watch from the back of the room.

"Do love with anger first," said Joan. "Concentrate.
Remember a situation in which you were really angry at a
girl you cared a lot about. Feel yourself becoming furious.
And then let's hear it!"

C.J. started racking his brain for something from his
past. He thought of Laurie, Sammie, and Jenna. Nothing
happened. He'd cared about them all, but he couldn't
remember ever being worked up about any one of them.
None had ever made him angry. He'd never allowed girls
to anger him. His mind drew a complete blank, and panic
began to take hold, gripping at his throat and threatening
to choke him.

Then he remembered Wendy. He had liked her well
enough, but she was getting too possessive, badgering him
all the time for his ring. One day he'd felt so cornered,
he'd wanted to just yell out, "I think you're great, okay? I
like you a lot! But please, please don't try and trap me!"

That would have to do.

C.J. looked at Emma, imagining her as Wendy. You're
crowding me, kid, he said to himself. Back off. He pic-
tured Wendy's gold locket, her pleading eyes, her hopeful
smile. Give me room, he thought. I need more space.

He concentrated as hard as he could, narrowed his eyes,
and then spat out, "I love you" for the first time ever. But
immediately he knew it wasn't right. It had caught in his
throat.

"No! No!" Joan called out with a trace of annoyance.
"What's that? That's not anger. That's . . . that's R2-D2."

The snickers that ran through the class ripped into C.J.'s soul. It felt like the whole world was laughing at him.

"Come on, C.J.," prodded Joan. "You're angry! Use that anger. Pretend Emma's cheated on you. She can't treat you like that. You've been as loyal as the day is long and you don't need to take that from her! No way! Give us that anger . . . that hurt . . . that love. I know it's complicated, so don't just use your eyes and voice. Put your body into it. . . ."

C.J. looked helplessly at Emma. She gave him a sympathetic smile and whispered, "Don't worry. I'd be peeing in my pants if I had to say that. Want me to say something awful to really tick you off?"

C.J. shook his head and shot Joan an angry glance to hide his embarrassment. She flashed him a sweet smile, sat down in her chair, and waited. A few of the kids began to whisper.

C.J. felt anger surge through him. His hands clenched in sweaty fists. This is too much, he thought. Just too damn much. Who does Joan think she is, anyway? She's probably never been in a major production in her whole life! What does she know?

Leaning forward to glare at Emma, he envisioned Joan before him. He stared at her quietly for a few seconds, breathing slowly and deeply.

The class grew silent.

Suddenly he stood up straight, dug his fists into the bottom of his pockets, and practically screamed, "I LOVE YOU!"

This time it felt real.

Everyone was silent. C.J. looked up at Joan expectantly. For a moment or two she looked around the class, then said quietly, "Any comments?"

No one raised a hand. Joan got up from the back of the class and began walking toward C.J. and Emma.

"C.J.," she began, "anger and love are a very complicated union. Anger means intense annoyance or tremendous fury, but love always implies caring as well. Most people only get very angry at people they care about." She turned to the class and continued. "The problem here is that I don't sense any of that caring. All I got was anger." Turning to C.J., she added, "You could have been yelling, 'TAKE OUT THE GARBAGE!' "

People began to laugh. C.J. noticed a girl wearing about ten silver bracelets on one arm cover her mouth and whisper something to the person next to her. They both giggled.

C.J. couldn't move. He was frozen in place. Emma reached out and put a hand gently on his arm. "Don't pay any attention," she whispered softly. "I thought it was excellent for a first try. I really did."

But C.J. didn't hear her. He only heard his own voice, and it kept yelling at him . . . with genuine anger: You can't act, you jerk! You're a fool . . . an impostor!

Slowly C.J. walked back to his chair, determined not to show the class how humiliated he felt. He concentrated on simply looking furious.

"C.J.," Joan called out. "You've got two more emotions to go. I think you can do it. Let's go for it, huh? Get back in the middle of the group."

C.J. spun on his heel until he faced her. "Okay, Joan," he said with a funny smile on his face. "I . . . I love you," he offered, going for the emotion of insincerity she had suggested earlier. He was genuinely insincere, and everything he did, right down to the "sexy" wink, made the point. Then, with a sarcastic smile to hide his embarrassment, C.J. plucked his jacket from the back of the chair, swung it casually over his shoulder, and sauntered out the door.

Joan turned to the class with a smile. "Now, that was good acting," she said triumphantly, but the door had already closed behind C.J. He never heard her.

C.J. began to run. He raced down the stairs and across

campus, praying that the registrar's office was open. Now that he was alone, his defenses were crumbling . . . and fast.

"This is it," he told himself. "I'm no actor. I'm just a rich kid with a rich old man and an even richer imagination. I couldn't act or sing my way out of a paper bag. Who the hell did I think I was kidding?"

Reaching the administration building in record time, C.J. yanked open the registrar's door. No one was there, but it didn't matter. He didn't need any help. All C.J. wanted was a blank piece of paper and a pen. The note would be simple: "Zed, I'm afraid this place just isn't for me. Thanks anyway. Charles J. Rollings."

Short and sweet. Very clean. He could be out of there by tonight.

Quickly he walked over to the receptionist's desk and reached for a pen. His eyes traveled over the profusion of envelopes and magazines, looking for a pad of paper. And then he saw it.

A check for five thousand dollars marked "gift" rested on top of the day's unopened mail. The signature at the bottom, in a familiar giant scrawl, was that of Charles B. Rollings, Sr. C.J. froze, his heart banging painfully in his chest.

His worst fears had become a reality.

✳ XII ✳

"**A**RE YOU SCARED?"

"Huh . . . what?" said Francesca, unwilling to let go of her daydream. She was still thinking about Marty and Eve striding off to their directing class together. Even though they loved to argue, they did seem so relaxed with each other. What does he want with me when it would be so easy to just fall into something with Eve? Francesca asked herself for the umpteenth time. How many times did he need her to put him off? Marty was bound to bring New York up again. She'd refuse, of course, but instinctively she knew it wouldn't make her happy. She had told herself trucking around New York City with Marty wasn't what SPAR was all about. The program was about work and improving her voice and honing her acting skills. But another voice inside her head had said, Francesca, you're a fool. You've got to face yourself sometime.

Marty's huge blue eyes swam before her, telling her she'd made a mistake. Then, suddenly, the person next to her again broke in.

"I said, are you scared . . . afraid . . . nervous?" the voice persisted.

"Scared?" repeated Francesca quizzically.

"Yeah. I'm terrified," said the sandy-haired boy.

"Of what?" asked Francesca in confusion, turning now to face him.

"Why . . . this class—vocal interpretation. It's an advanced voice class. Maybe I should have signed up for intermediate."

"Oh . . ." Francesca responded absentmindedly. Her mind was still far away. Marty really did have the most amazing eyes . . . not to mention the sexiest body . . . so solid and powerful.

"Right . . . advanced voice," she said, forcing herself back to the present. "No, I'm not particularly scared. At least not about the voice part. I've never done interpretive work, but it can't be that hard."

"Have you been studying voice for long?"

"Ummmmm . . . about ten years."

"Wow . . . that is a long time! I just started in the eighth grade," said the boy mournfully. "I knew I shouldn't be in this class. I don't know what I was thinking about when I signed up." His open, friendly face seemed so sad. He fidgeted nervously. Francesca wished she could think of some way to comfort him, but she couldn't.

"By the way, I'm Theodore Willis," he said.

"Nice to meet you. I'm Francesca Minelli," whispered Francesca just as Lilly, the voice teacher, walked through the door. Francesca was glad Lilly was her teacher. She'd seemed so nice at the opening ceremony. This was going to be a great way to start off at SPAR—in a class she was good in with a teacher she liked.

Lilly had on a faded lavender sweater and black pants that hung comfortably on her neat, graceful figure. She smiled sweetly at the class and everyone fell silent.

"I presume everyone is warmed up," she said matter-of-factly.

No one moved. Warmed up! thought Francesca. We just got here. Of course we're not warmed up.

"No?" said Lilly, calmly looking out over the silent, frightened faces. "Well, today I forgive you as it's our first class together. But in the future, I expect you warmed up and ready to go. We only have fifty minutes of class time and I don't want to take it up with basics. This is an advanced voice class. Let's not forget."

Francesca shifted her weight. Wow! Lilly was tough. This class was really going to hop. She glanced at Theodore, who was staring a hole in the floor at his feet.

"Okay, let's all stand up," said Lilly in her soft yet commanding voice. The class leaped to its feet. "Let's run through a few scales to start with."

After a few minutes of workout, Francesca felt her vocal chords begin to warm and stretch. It felt good.

"And now let's go through the vowels," said Lilly, and again the room burst into cacophony as everyone aed and eed and oed.

"Exaggerate! Really exaggerate! I want to see those muscles move. Open your mouths! Stretch." Lilly walked from one student to the next as she issued her orders. Francesca could feel her facial muscles extend to the limit, stretch and loosen. She was ready to sing.

"Okay. That's more like it," said Lilly, returning to the front of the class. "Now, I thought we'd start off with some duets." Nervous giggles washed through the classroom. "I thought you'd agree." She consulted the list of names on her desk. "Abby and Carl to the front, please."

Francesca leaned forward excitedly and reset the tortoiseshell combs in her hair. She'd never worked specifically on duets before. Something new. This could be fun.

Abby and Carl were assigned a song from *Cabaret*. Francesca thought they did okay, but Abby's voice wasn't very strong. It didn't seem to project like it should. Maybe she was just nervous being the first one called up. Carl had a nice tenor. The next couple was better, but Francesca still felt confident in her own abilities. She'd had good training over the years. It was about to pay off.

Theodore was called to the front with her, and followed mournfully at her heels.

"I'd like you two to sing 'One Hand, One Heart' from *West Side Story*," said Lilly. "It's on page three of the songbook. . . . And remember, the two of you are in love. I want to feel that." She nodded to the pianist to begin the accompaniment. Francesca glanced quickly at the music. A love song. It wasn't a part she'd sung before, but that didn't matter. What did Lilly mean, she wanted to "feel" Francesca and Theodore in love? It looked pretty straightforward. Francesca shrugged. She could handle it. Lilly's comment was probably just a throwaway.

They started off a little shaky, but quickly got it together. It felt good to sing, to feel her voice explore the notes and then soar with them. And Theodore had an excellent voice. She couldn't believe he'd been so nervous. Their voices melded in perfect harmony. She wished the song could have gone on a lot longer.

"Okay, class, I think we might as well get comfortable with each other," said Lilly when the final notes died away. Francesca felt flushed and exhilarated. "Let's start talking. Give this couple some feedback, please."

"I think Francesca has a wonderful voice," sighed a girl from the back of the room.

"Me, too," agreed another. "It's so clear."

"The perfect complement to Theodore's bass," came another.

Francesca could feel her face burn with embarrassment. She glanced over at Theodore, who was grinning from ear to ear. If only they could sing and sit down, and not have to remain on center stage. This is what frightened her so about performing. About acting. Francesca squared her shoulders. She had to get over the fear. She absolutely had to.

"Well . . ." said Lilly slowly, standing up. "I agree with the class. You both have technically very proficient voices. I'm impressed."

Francesca let her breath out slowly with relief.

"But," continued Lilly, "if you were trying out for a play I was directing, you wouldn't make it."

Francesca fought hard to keep her jaw from dropping. What was Lilly saying? She'd heard her own voice. She'd been trained to hear it. And it was good. Very good, in fact.

"Technical ability is only a small fraction of the total picture in musical theater. On a bigger scale, you've got to relate—to the person you're singing with, to the plot, and, most importantly, to the audience. The only way they're going to feel the emotion of the song, of the story you're trying to tell, is if you put it there." She walked back to her seat. "So let's take it from the top again. Project the emotion of this song. I want to feel your love for each other."

The blood drained slowly from Francesca's face. What did she mean, "relate"? Wasn't the blending of two voices relating enough? She looked at Theodore, but he seemed perfectly in control of the situation. Not confused at all. The pianist struck up the first notes. Theodore's eyes held hers in a gaze that made Francesca want to run from the room. It was a look that said they'd been to bed and back.

Uncomfortably warm, Francesca nervously pulled a rubber band out of her jeans pocket to make a ponytail out of her long, thick hair. Her neck felt damp.

And then it was time. Turning to Theodore, Francesca opened her mouth to sing . . . and moments later felt panic set in. Her clear, sweet voice had disappeared. In its place was a thin, uninspired sound. Frantically, she tried to find her usual rich tone, but it was gone. Halfway through the

song, when undying love is declared between the two
characters, Theodore reached for her hands and held them
tenderly, but Francesca tensed and pulled back uncon-
sciously. Her voice began to warble, the way it had during
her first recital years ago. Tears threatened, but she blinked
them back.

"No . . . stop!" ordered Lilly firmly. The piano fell
silent. "Francesca, respond to Theodore. When he looks
you in the eye, look him back. When he reaches for you,
be there for him. Right now you don't look like you're
even on the same stage with him. Give him something to
work with. You're supposed to be in love with him. Show
me that love. I want sweaty palms and heaving breasts.
The whole bit."

Francesca stared at the floor, thoroughly mortified. Her
knees threatened to collapse under her. Sweaty palms!
Heaving breasts! How could Lilly talk like that? What did
she want? A Francesca, Damian scene?! In public? It was
frightening enough in private. A confusion that had nothing
to do with music and song. Francesca fought hard to get
herself under control. She had to. If she couldn't handle
this class, the rest of SPAR was down the tubes, too.

They tried again, but when Francesca started to reach
out to Theodore, she felt like a mime coming up against an
invisible wall. It was as if a barrier were holding her back.

The bell announcing the end of class jangled her nerves
even further. Slowly she gathered up her things and started
out the door. She couldn't bear to look any of her classmates in the eye. She'd failed. She'd sauntered confidently
into an advanced voice class, and now they all knew she
was really a novice.

"May I see you a moment, Francesca . . . in my office," said Lilly quietly, resting her hand gently on Francesca's shoulder.

Francesca felt her stomach turn over and over as she
followed Lilly down the hall. What was she going to say?

That Francesca shouldn't be part of SPAR at all? That her being there must be some kind of gross mistake . . . a huge joke?

"Francesca, talk to me," Lilly began when she'd closed the door. "What's going on in your head? What's holding you back?"

"I don't know," said Francesca mournfully. "This has never happened before."

"Have you done interpretive work before?"

"No," replied Francesca, "but I've been studying voice for more than half my life . . . since I was a kid."

"Your voice, per se, isn't the problem," explained Lilly gently. "Your voice is obviously a finely polished tool, but now you've got to fine-tune the rest of your approach to carry out the emotion behind the words you're singing. Do you understand what I'm saying?"

Francesca nodded.

"In musical comedy or opera or even for the rock stars, it's not only technical proficiency that gets them to the top," continued Lilly. "A lot of people have that. But they . . . and you . . . have to be able to sell something . . . to sell yourself. You've got to convey to the audience the emotion behind the song, or the whole plot becomes meaningless."

"Where do I start?" asked Francesca, fearing she would have to redo the years of training. It seemed like an impossible task.

"You have to start with the person and her situation. Be that person, feel as she feels, and then use everything you've got to put it across—your body, your mind, your voice."

Francesca nodded again.

"Tell me, how well do you relate to other people . . . your classmates, for instance?" Lilly said after a slight hesitation.

"Okay . . . I guess," said Francesca with surprise. What a strange question.

"Do you go out and do things with other people . . . silly things . . . serious things?"

"Yes. I have friends back home. And here." Francesca replied, completely mystified. "I've never had lots of time, though, really. I've always worked pretty hard on my voice. My brothers and sisters and I are very close. We did a lot together."

"Aha!" said Lilly triumphantly. "That could be the problem. Too much work, too much time with your brothers and sisters, and not quite enough experience with friends . . . and the opposite sex?"

"I'm not totally inexperienced," protested Francesca weakly. "I like my friends; and I've dated a little, but I enjoy my family and—"

"Of course you do. But you all know each other so well and understand each other that there's no need to take any emotional risks. No one would say anything to hurt you, and you don't have to explore with them how they feel, because you probably just know . . . right?"

Francesca smiled. Well, Lilly sure hit the nail on the head. She never confided in her friends. Actually, she rarely confided in anyone, though sometimes she'd reveal things to her sisters. "I suppose you're right. For the most part we've always understood each other," she said quietly. She was still confused, but there was more light now than darkness. Things were beginning to make sense.

"You see," Lilly explained patiently, "when you get up to play a role onstage, you're taking an emotional risk. You have to give of yourself mentally, technically, and physically . . . and then be judged on it by a group of strangers—the audience. It can be shattering, but it can be just as wonderful, too, when you make that investment and it works."

"That's where the standing ovation comes in, huh?" joked Francesca.

Lilly laughed. "You've got it! But you have to work for moments like that. Work like you've never worked before—giving yourself to that audience. Do you think you'll be able to do that?"

"So what you're saying is, I need to walk down Main Street in Lowell and talk to strangers . . . make myself relate . . . learn to open up."

Lilly laughed again. "Well, you might get carted away to the funny farm, but that's the idea. I suggest you just start with your classmates, though. Sit with new people every meal. Feel yourself reaching out to them."

Lilly paused a moment, her eyes studying Francesca's face, as if to decide whether or not the frightened young woman could deal with her final thoughts. Francesca stared back expectantly . . . nervously . . . and finally Lilly spoke.

"You know, Francesca, I noticed you signed up for the first talent contest in an ensemble number. What I'm teaching in this class is just what you need to know to pull off whatever you're doing. If it's not a question of relating to your fellow performers, then it's a matter of relating to your own part emotionally. I don't want to add to your anxiety, but you've got to 'feel' what you do . . . completely. If you don't, you really won't be doing yourself or your part justice."

Francesca swallowed hard. Lilly was asking a lot of her. Opening up to people was not one of her strong points. And trying to relate to Iris was nearly impossible. She turned to Lilly and smiled.

"I guess all I can do is try."

"That's all I'm asking of you," Lilly replied quietly. "Now I have another class. You can stay here and think about what we've discussed if you like." And with that, she was gone.

Francesca sat in Lilly's office for a few minutes, trying to let everything she'd been told sink in. Finally she stood up and put on her coat. If I'm supposed to relate better, maybe I should start with Marty, since he seems to be my biggest problem, she said to herself. Francesca wandered off to her second-period class in a daze. She felt like Alice in Wonderland about to enter a whole new world.

✳ XIII ✳

C.J. STARED AT HIS FATHER'S FAMILIAR SIGNATURE scrawled across the bottom of the check. It was big and bold, dominating the whole check—dominating everything, C.J. thought, even his only son at a distance of two thousand miles. C.J. was rooted to the spot. He began to tremble. So it was true! His father had bought him his spot at SPAR! How long could that remain a secret, especially if he kept botching classes like he just had?

C.J. desperately tried to take a deep breath, certain it would help him think more clearly, but his shallow breaths persisted, and his chest began to tighten. Panic seized him. Moments later he ran out of the office, only one purpose in mind.

He raced across campus, up the three flights of MacCready, and into his room. Grabbing his suitcase from the closet, he began throwing in his belongings. Soon the room was a wreck, with clothes everywhere, drawers opened, books strewn across the floor.

Suddenly the door flew open.

"The paint finally came in," said Michael cheerfully,

swinging a gallon of blue paint in each hand. "What the—!" He stared openmouthed.

"I'm leaving, Michael," said C.J., gathering up the books.

"Things went so well with Serena Friday night," joked Michael, "you're running off to Niagara Falls to get married . . . right?"

"This isn't a joke, Michael," barked C.J.

Michael slowly lowered the paint to the floor and sat down on his bed, the one clean place left in the room.

"So . . . what's happening?" he asked quietly.

C.J. hesitated. Maybe he ought to tell Michael. Maybe it would help to tell someone. But when he opened his mouth to speak, a sob caught in his throat. All at once he had the urge to cry, to throw himself on his bed and cry and cry until there was no more pain left. He forced his attention back to his packing. Crying in front of another guy would never do.

"Hey, talk to me, man. Your face looks like a funeral procession," continued Michael. "What's going on?"

"Nothing. I just decided this joint isn't for me. I don't need to spend a year of my life being pushed around by Broadway has-beens. If I want to act, I can go to New York and get a job just like that." He snapped his fingers to make the point.

"Well, hell, let's go together," said Michael. "I think we could have a blast. I haven't known you too long, but I like you, Tex. Of course, you take yourself a little too seriously, but I reckon New York would knock that out of you pretty quick."

C.J. shot Michael a dark look, but the expression on Michael's face pulled him up short. Michael wasn't being flip. Michael was being serious . . . and caring. His face was wreathed in concern. C.J. swallowed hard.

"I'm not going to New York, Michael. I'm going back . . . back home."

Michael was silent for a moment. "Family problems?"

"I guess you could say so," said C.J., not trusting himself to look Michael in the eye.

"I'm sorry, man," said Michael quietly. "I really am. Want to talk about it?"

Again C.J. felt tempted to confide in Michael, but again he held back. He wasn't used to close friends. People usually liked him because of his money. He didn't know how to handle genuine kindness . . . or any real emotion, for that matter. That's what had first drawn him to acting. Onstage he could act out any emotion he wanted, be anyone he wanted, get as close to people as he wanted, and everyone just thought he was a great actor. Well, he was . . . maybe. But sometimes he wasn't sure where reality ended and acting began. He hadn't worked that one out yet.

"Was there a death in the family?" probed Michael gently.

"I suppose there was," replied C.J. absentmindedly.

"Your dad?"

"No . . . mine." The words just slipped out, and C.J. went back to his packing. He felt strange, like he was a fly on the wall, watching himself move around. He felt detached, and for a moment he wondered why he was even bothering to pack. Why not just walk out to the highway, stick out his thumb, and end up somewhere his father would never find him?

"Yours? Man, you aren't making a lot of sense," said Michael, his voice laced with worry. "I think you ought to talk to me . . . now."

C.J. let Michael take him by the shoulders and sit him down. Again, it didn't even feel like him. He felt he was watching Michael sit this stranger down.

"Something big and scary's going on in your head," began Michael, "and I don't think you should be left alone with it. Now . . . shoot."

C.J. sat staring at the floor for a long, long time. Finally, without looking up, he said, "My father bought me my place at SPAR."

"Huh—!" said Michael. "What do you mean, 'he bought you your place'?"

"I mean, he shelled out big bucks so this place would take me. I'm here because I'm rich, not because I have any talent. And," he added with a sarcastic grin, "I must admit, it kind of bothers me a little. Know what I mean?"

"Hang on," said Michael, looking C.J. directly in the eyes. "How do you know all this?"

"I saw the check . . . in the registrar's office."

"And in the lower left corner where you scribble in what a check's for, it said, 'bribe,' right?" Michael's tone was pushy but patient.

"Don't be crazy; of course not. But why else would my dad be sending SPAR a check for five thousand dollars?"

"Books?" asked Michael. "Tuition?"

"That was paid ages ago," replied C.J. despondently.

"Well, why don't you call him and ask him?" suggested Michael.

"You don't know my dad," C.J. said, wringing his hands in despair.

"Well, you're right about that," remarked Michael. "But what can he say? What can he do to you?"

"Disinherit me."

"Big deal. I thought we were going to New York and become famous actors anyway. Who needs his money?"

C.J. laughed uncertainly. Michael could really be so naive sometimes. Life was so easy for this guy. Didn't he know money meant power? That it could make things happen? Or maybe, C.J. thought with a grimace, Michael never needed money to succeed. He had another calling card. Talent.

"Seems to me you've got nothing to lose by at least

giving your father a call,'' continued Michael. ''If he gets heavy with you . . . hang up!''

C.J. shook his head. Michael was wild. C.J. couldn't even imagine hanging up on his old man. A person didn't do that to Charles Rollings, Sr. He was just too important for that. Too imposing. Awesome.

''Hey, what were you doing snooping around the registrar's office anyway?'' asked Michael.

''I wasn't snooping,'' said C.J. defensively.

''You just thought you'd make a few extra bucks cleaning up the administrative offices,'' quipped Michael.

C.J. laughed again, then sobered. ''No, I was about to write a letter to Zed telling him I was leaving.''

''You mean you were going to quit even before you saw the check?'' asked Michael.

''Yeah, I guess I was. Let's just say acting class didn't go too well this morning,'' C.J. said, concentrating on the floor again. ''I realize I just don't have what it takes.''

''You wouldn't be here if you weren't good,'' protested Michael.

''Tell that to Joan,'' barked C.J.

''Joan! You didn't have her at eight o'clock this morning by any chance, did you?''

''Yeah . . . why?''

''Were you asked to say 'I love you' three different ways?''

''Yeah. . . . How did you know?''

''Because I have a friend in that class who was telling me all about it—'' began Michael.

''And he told you he was laughing about the jerk in his acting class, right?''

''Wrong! Totally wrong.''

C.J. looked up at Michael in confusion.

''He just told me how some guy had had trouble saying 'I love you' with anger and caring all at the same time. Then—did you leave class early or something?''

"Yeah, I got so pissed off, I left."

"Okay. That jibes. So he said the teacher asked you to say 'I love you' with insincerity, and you looked the teacher right in the eye and told her you loved her. Afterwards she said she'd never seen such insincerity in all her life. She thought you were good—only you never heard that because you'd already walked out."

"She . . . what? She did?!" stuttered C.J.

"Man, you did okay. Believe me!"

C.J. stood up, trying to keep the smile off his face. A surge of energy went through him. "She thought I was pretty good, huh?" he kept repeating as he wandered around the room. Suddenly he sat down hard. What if Michael's friend was exaggerating, he thought. Joan sure didn't seem impressed with my acting at all. And it's the Joans at this place I have to impress, not some wide-eyed kid. Still, maybe I did do okay . . . maybe.

"So now that that's cleared up, why not give the old man a ring and find out about that check," Michael suggested, interrupting C.J.'s private battle.

C.J. stared at his roommate. "He never listens to me, Michael. What's the point?"

"Make him listen to you. Try a different approach. I don't know what you've been using, but find another way!" Michael banged his fist on the table for emphasis.

C.J. sat still for a few minutes. Suddenly he got up. "Okay. Okay, Michael. I'll call him." He turned to his roommate, one hand on the door. "But if this doesn't work out, I'm hopping a freighter to the Amazon rain forests."

As he closed the door behind him, C.J. wondered if he shouldn't just buy his ticket right then and there. . . .

❋ XIV ❋

"**I** DON'T KNOW WHAT MADE YOU CHANGE YOUR MIND," said Marty, helping Francesca off the train at Grand Central Station, "but I'm sure glad you did. I've been really looking forward to this."

Francesca smiled weakly at him. She knew very well what had made her change her mind—her talk with Lilly earlier in the week—but she still wasn't sure going to New York for an entire Saturday afternoon with Marty was the best idea in the world. She had to admit she was pretty excited about seeing the city, but she was plenty nervous about Marty's growing effect on her.

"Let's walk down Fifth Avenue to the Empire State Building," suggested Marty. "That way you can get a bit of a feel for the city."

Francesca didn't protest when he took her hand. There were people everywhere, some of whom looked friendly, and others decidedly not. It felt safe holding hands.

A few minutes later, with the thick crowds of Forty-second Street behind them, Francesca was able to take in the New York City street life. Marty's hand felt wonderful— warm and strong and protective. It made her forget her fears about this wild city she knew mostly from the crime columns in the newspaper. Francesca glanced at Marty and felt a thrilling jolt of electricity shoot through her body. The feeling scared her. She'd experienced it before with him, though she hadn't wanted to admit it. Also Damian. Francesca forced herself to contain the stirrings within her. They've gotten me into a mess before . . . but they never will again, she thought. Filled with determination, Francesca feigned interest in the huge skyscrapers.

"Is it like this where you live?" asked Francesca, willing herself to concentrate on the huge buildings towering above them. They were beautiful in an overwhelming sort of way. "Boston has skyscrapers, too. But not like this!"

Marty laughed. Francesca loved his laugh. It came from somewhere way down deep inside him and seemed to embrace her. It was as if it said, "Don't worry. Things will be fine." Francesca felt herself relaxing.

"Not quite," continued Marty. "My old neighborhood is mostly dinky little houses on dinky little streets decorated with the occasional rusty car sitting up on cement blocks with no wheels."

"What happened to them?" asked Francesca innocently.

Again Marty laughed. "Someone was dumb enough to leave their car unattended. The hoods out there can strip a car in no time flat. Wheels, tires, battery, mirrors, all gone by the time you go in and buy a quart of milk. Some parts of Brooklyn are no picnic, that's for sure."

"Must have been a pretty tough place to grow up," said Francesca seriously.

"It was interesting," said Marty quietly, "and I think it gave me a lot of insight into human nature. I mean, things were pretty basic where I grew up."

Francesca looked at Marty with new respect. The wind was tossing his dark curls dramatically around his face. Too bad he was going to settle for the behind-the-scenes job of director. He would be such a powerful presence as an actor, she thought. He exuded an indefinable quality that made him stand out from the crowds. Kind of like Dustin Hoffman. Marty was a winner. He was serious and convinced about himself and his abilities. Maybe that's what made him seem so intense. Somehow, knowing this made her feel less frightened of him. All at once Francesca felt that she understood what Lilly meant about relating—opening up to another person so you could begin to understand each other. She thought she was beginning to understand Marty.

"Maybe that's why I want to be a director," said Marty, his voice seeming to come from miles away. "So I can have control over things. So I can create a world the way I want it. I'm tired of being told how it has to be. Like my father. He's a plumber, and I love him a lot, and he's very hardworking, but his dream for me is to head up my own construction company. That's his vision of success. But it's not mine."

Francesca stopped walking and turned to Marty. "I admire what you're doing." She squeezed his hand. It was an intimate thing to do, but it felt right. "I know it would have been easier to just do what everyone expected, instead of what you want."

"Not for me." Marty shook his head. "I knew I wanted out a long time ago," he said fiercely. "It would have been harder to stay. It was just a question of finding a way out. That's why this year at SPAR is so important to me. I've got to make it. It's my first step out of Brooklyn, and I never want to go back. But I've also got to prove to my dad that I can make it in the theater. Right now he thinks it's a cop-out."

Francesca stared at him, both awed and thrilled by his intensity. So many guys she knew didn't have a clue what it was all about; what they wanted to do with their lives. But Marty seemed so sure of himself . . . so mature. Another shiver ran down her spine. Her body tingled with a rush of adrenaline. If only she could just throw her arms around him, hold him close for a second. What could be so bad about that? It wouldn't mean she'd lose control. Probably he wouldn't, either. They wouldn't have to be involved. Casual affection. That's all. But even as she thought this, warning signals began to go off in her head. If she hugged him now, would he expect more later? Where would it all end? Subconciously she drew back from him, jamming both hands deep into her pockets.

They spent the next hour window-shopping and people-watching in comfortable silence. Finally Marty came to a stop.

"Okay," he said, standing in the middle of the sidewalk and looking up. "The Empire State Building, madam. What do you think?

Francesca followed his gaze up and up . . . and up, then sucked in her breath. The building seemed to go on forever, its top rooted more in the heavens than the earth.

"Wow," she said, letting her breath out slowly. "That's it, huh? The famous Empire State Building. It's really something."

"And wait till you see the view from the top," said Marty excitedly, leading her through the revolving doors.

Francesca followed in a daze from one elevator to the next, and finally they were stepping out into the brisk wind of the observation deck. They were the only ones there and the wind howled gently in the quiet. From far, far away, an occasional horn sounded. Marty started to lead her over to the edge, but Francesca held back. She didn't care if there was a wire fence all around, looking down on New York from eighty-eight stories up was going to take some getting used to.

"Don't be scared," said Marty. "I promise not to let you go." He put his arm around her shoulders.

When Francesca finally got the nerve to open her eyes and look out, she was stunned into silence. It was beautiful. Absolutely breathtaking. The sun was going down over the Hudson River, making New Jersey on the other side a golden haze. The buildings below were sharp contrasts of light and dark, and all the windows on the east side glowed like molten gold.

"Unbelievable, isn't it?" Marty sighed, then added softly, "But then, so are you, Francesca."

Francesca felt the blood rush to her face. Not trusting herself to say anything, she stole a look at Marty from behind her curtain of hair. The rich light from the setting sun highlighted the strong planes of his face, making him seem so much older, and terribly, wonderfully masculine. Francesca swallowed hard. She couldn't deny her feelings for him. There was something about him she wanted to be near. All she could think of was how wonderful it would feel to have his arms holding her tightly to his chest. But she also couldn't deny that it was just these feelings that scared her to death. Things have to move more slowly, so I can feel my way along, she thought. Maybe a friendship would be best at first. It would be so easy to give in . . . totally. But I'm not ready for that. Damian was proof.

Suddenly, as if he'd read her thoughts, Marty pulled her in closer to his side, and held her firmly but gently.

She could feel his taut muscles line up perfectly with the curve of her hip. Again she wrestled with her conflicting emotions. Why couldn't she just tell him what she was feeling—that he was driving her absolutely wild, but that she needed his help to keep things from getting out of hand . . . and enjoy it all? She sucked in her breath slowly, trying desperately for control. Marty ran a finger softly down the side of her face. Suddenly, something snapped in Francesca.

"I . . . I think we should head back to Lowell," she stammered, pulling away from him. She wanted out. Things were getting too crazy and she didn't know how to handle it anymore. She never did. She'd related enough for one day.

"You know, Francesca," Marty began, ignoring her suggestion and renewing his hold, "when I was a little kid, I used to love coming up here with my dad. It used to make me feel powerful—like I could do or be anything. I would imagine that I was some kind of superhero and that any second I'd see a disaster. I had it all planned. I'd spring into action, run into the stairwell over there and change into my Superlion costume, then fly off to save everyone."

"Superlion!" Francesca began to giggle despite her near panic. "Superlion. What were you planning to do? Growl at everyone?"

Marty burst out laughing. "Are you making fun of me? Don't you think that's a little unkind? I mean, we hardly know each other!"

"No . . . oh, no!" Francesca smiled affectionately. "I think Superlion is adorable. I love the whole idea."

She was beginning to feel okay again. The atmosphere between them had lightened considerably. She pulled her jacket in close against the evening chill and looked out over the city. Lights were beginning to blink on here and there like fireflies.

Suddenly she felt Marty playfully nuzzle her neck. Francesca stiffened. Quickly she moved away, tucking her windblown hair behind her ears. She hoped he wouldn't notice her shaking hands. "I've got to get back now, Marty. Really. I have to practice," she said, trying to keep her voice even.

"What's wrong?" Marty snapped, suddenly annoyed and embarrassed. "Is laughing something you Boston girls think is beneath you?"

Francesca lowered her head, hoping to hide the tears in her eyes. "No . . . no. I like to laugh."

"Then what is it?" Marty persisted, hunching his shoulders against the wind. "Why are you so jumpy? Ever since we got up here, you've been trying to get away from me. What's wrong?"

"I . . . I . . . I can't," Francesca stammered.

"You can't laugh? Of course you can." Marty cupped her face in his hands and looked intently down at her.

Francesca felt like a trapped animal. The afternoon had been so wonderful . . . such fun. It had been so nice to be with a boy, one she felt she could really care for— maybe even trust. But things were going too fast now. She couldn't keep up. She glanced at his face. It was so close. Suddenly Francesca whirled around and ran for the door that led to the elevator. She dodged past a young couple just getting off the elevator, and was lunging for the door handle when Marty caught up with her. Grabbing her arm, he pulled her into the corner.

"Don't run away, Francesca . . . please. Talk to me. Tell me what's wrong! Is it something I said, something I did?" He stood with a hand on each of her shoulders so she couldn't escape. Francesca tried to find words, but couldn't. Nothing made sense right now.

Marty gave her a minute, then said firmly, "Listen. I've got all evening, all night if you need it, but we're not leaving this spot until you tell me what's going on."

Francesca glared at Marty silently and tried to push past him, but he held her back. Tears of anger and confusion spilled onto her cheeks. Marty's hands slipped from her shoulders.

"Look. Maybe I made a mistake," he said quietly. "I don't know. But where I come from, touching a girl is, well, no big deal. That doesn't mean it's that way for everyone. So maybe I shouldn't have." He paused, then brought her face up gently so they were looking each other in the eye. "Was that it? Did I move too fast for you?"

Francesca nodded slowly and looked down again. "I'd like to be friends with you, Marty. I . . . I really would, but I don't know if I'm ready for anything romantic." She glanced at him through her tears. "I'm sorry . . ."

"Shhhhh . . ." said Marty, putting a finger gently to her lips. "You don't have to apologize. I understand." He hesitated. "I'll try to understand. If it's friendship you want, then let's be friends. The best ever! Okay?"

Francesca was so relieved, she threw her arms around his neck. He did understand. She could feel it. He wasn't just feeding her a line. Then—and even weeks after, she couldn't explain how it happened, or who started it—their lips found each other and held, until the most wonderful feeling in the world warmed her all the way through to her chilly toes.

✳ XV ✳

MONDAY; EARLY AFTERNOON, C.J. STARED AT THE phone, a mixture of fear and frustration causing him to hesitate. He'd tried calling his father every day for almost a week, but hadn't been able to get through. There was a different excuse every time: "I'm sorry, but Mr. Rollings is out of town for a few days." "No, Mr. Rollings is golfing this afternoon." "I'm sorry, he's in conference." His father's new secretary hadn't recognized C.J.'s voice, and he'd declined to leave a message. C.J. wanted to catch his father off guard. The call had to come from him. C.J. grimaced.

Tomorrow he had to either face Joan again in acting class or decide to finally leave SPAR. The program was into its third week, and he couldn't force himself any longer to drag through classes not knowing if his talent or his dad's money had gotten him there. The strain was killing him.

He had to reach his father today. Time had run out.

C.J. dialed the familiar Dallas number once again, gave his credit card number, and then listened to the phone ring and ring . . . and ring.

"Dad!" C.J. almost dropped the phone. "What are you doing answering your own phones?"

"Hello, Son," boomed his father's friendly voice. "The secretary just took off sick and everyone else seems to be out to lunch, so I promoted myself to receptionist." His father's familiar deep laugh filled C.J. with apprehension. It was so confident. So sure. "How are things going out there? You haven't fallen in love with some East Coast prude, now have you?" Again, the powerful laughter. C.J. could feel his resolve begin to crumble. Next to his father, he felt like a timid mouse.

"Need some more money?" asked Mr. Rollings when C.J. didn't laugh at his joke. "Just tell me how much and I'll have it to you by later this afternoon."

Something snapped in C.J.'s head. He saw the check lying on the registrar's desk with his father's bold signature, and suddenly his fear took a back seat. He had to know the truth.

"Dad, I want to talk to you about something."

"Sure, Son, fire away. I've got a meeting in five minutes, but that should give us plenty of time. What's the problem?"

C.J. hesitated. Five minutes was nothing. His father was always moving through life in fifth gear. C.J. wondered if he ever slowed up long enough to think about where he was going.

"You haven't knocked some girl up, have you?" asked his father, responding to C.J.'s silence. "Nothing like that, I hope."

"No, Dad. Nothing like that. I wanted to talk to you about money."

"Money! My favorite subject. You haven't gone through that bank account I set up for you out there already, have you? Not that I mind. You know that."

"Dad! Be quiet . . . please . . . for one moment. I *have* to talk to you. NOW!"

"Sure . . . Son," his father said hesitantly. "Go ahead. I'm all ears."

All at once panic hit C.J. His father's meeting started in three minutes. Not enough time to discuss the problem. Maybe he should tell him to forget it or invent some stupid problem that they could discuss in three minutes, like what kind of car he should buy. His dad was bound to make a quick decision on that.

"Son?"

"I'm still here. But your meeting . . ."

"Tell me what's on your mind. Forget the meeting. It can wait. You're my boy."

C.J. felt tears sting his eyes. He couldn't remember the last time he'd heard his father speak like that. He actually sounded interested in what C.J. had to say.

"I . . . I just wanted to ask you a question," began C.J. swallowing hard.

His father was silent . . . and it was terrifying. C.J. wasn't used to demanding this kind of attention—or taking a stand. He took a deep breath. It was now or never. If he didn't set the record straight in the next few minutes, C.J. was sure he never would. . . .

"Dad . . . did you . . . did you buy my place here at SPAR?" C.J. blurted out.

"C.J.! What on earth made you think that?"

"I saw . . . a check . . . in the registrar's office . . . from you . . . five thousand dollars. Was it a bribe . . . to get me in here?" C.J. had to force each word out. The pain of it left him breathless.

"Son . . . would I do that?!" began his father.

"Yes, Dad, you would . . . you have. Remember how I got into swanky old St. Andrew's School. You know I didn't have the grades for that place."

"But you were smart enough," protested his dad. "I believed in you. I knew once you were in, you'd shine

. . . and you did. Money is made to smooth out life's rocky roads.''

"Well, I don't want you smoothing out mine anymore, Dad. I want to do it on my own. Okay?''

"Well, okay, Son. I guess you're old enough to make your own decisions, but I . . .''

"The first decision I'm making is to get out of this place,'' interrupted C.J., feeling more certain of himself now. His dad had admitted he was wrong. Or at least, almost.

"Oh, Son, don't do that.'' His dad's obvious disappointment shocked C.J. His dad had never seemed interested in his theater career before. "You're good. You could be a great actor. It's what you want to do, isn't it?''

"Not if I only get ahead on your bribes . . .'' shouted C.J., suddenly out of control.

"Son, you were chosen for SPAR on your own merit.''

"What about that check?'' demanded C.J., shaking with renewed anger.

"I was making a contribution.'' His voice remained calm. "I imagine all the parents will. We just got a letter in the mail outlining their expenses since the new Kenner Center was put up, and they were running short. Naturally, I gave something.''

C.J.'s head was buzzing. It wasn't a bribe, just a lousy contribution that had kept him up almost every night for the past week! C.J. wanted to laugh from relief.

"Look, Son,'' C.J.'s father began hesitantly, "I know I've . . . well . . . been maybe a little overinvolved with your life. I have money. I want to make things easy for you.'' He coughed nervously.

"Ah, Dad,'' said C.J., feeling a little sheepish for accusing his father of foul play. "I should have know you wouldn't . . .''

"No, now you listen to me,'' his father interrupted sternly. "I'm not real good when it comes to expressing feelings. Never have been. But I'm going to try now, and I want you to listen."

C.J. was stunned. His father rarely chose to talk. He was a man of action. Too much action, in fact.

"I've spoiled you," continued his father, "thinking I was making things right for you. Looks like it's been all wrong."

"No, Dad, please don't blame yourself," begged C.J. "I could've refused. It's not all your fault."

"Yes it is, because I'm telling you it is. I'm still your father."

They both laughed nervously.

"When I was your age, I didn't have fifteen cents to my name. When I was about twenty, I decided to change all that. I've worked hard for a long time, but it's been worth it . . . in a way. Everything I have today comes from that hard work."

C.J. felt tears once again welling in his eyes. He hadn't expected his dad to open up so much. He never had.

"But, Son, your hard work got you into SPAR, not me. You've got a heck of a lot of talent. You damn well stay in Lowell and knock those people dead. You can do it."

C.J.'s ears were ringing. His dad thought he had talent! How come he'd never said so before?

"Funny thing," continued his dad with a strange laugh. "All your life, I've been trying to shield you from needs . . . from wants . . . with money. But maybe we both learned something from this experience. After you left home this month, I realized I was much happier having you around. I'm not rich without you . . . not one bit. So, well, let's talk. Let's keep talkin'. I think you need me as much as I need you."

"I do . . ." began C.J., clutching the receiver tightly in the cramped phone booth. "I want to be able to—"

Suddenly the secretary broke in on the line. "I'm terribly sorry Mr. Rollings, but the meeting's started and they need you. Mr. Rogers has a flight back to Chicago in an hour that he has to be on, and he wants to conclude the offshore drilling contract before he goes.''

"Damn!" whispered Mr. Rollings. "Son, excuse me. I've got to go. This contract is worth millions and old Rogers can be a bear if he's kept waiting.''

"Sure, Dad. No problem," said C.J., feeling like someone had just popped the biggest balloon he'd ever floated on in his life.

"We'll talk later . . . okay? Check with my secretary.''

"Okay," C.J. replied, then he hesitated. "I love you.''

"Me, too," replied his father almost gruffly, and then the line went dead.

C.J. hung the phone back on the hook with a sad smile. It was a good talk, but he had wanted more. Then for a second he laughed out loud. Too bad Joan missed my parting line, he thought. I wonder what she'd have thought of that!

It wasn't until later that evening that a sobered C.J. realized the phone call was not enough. He still had something to prove, and the talent contest looked like the only place to do it. . . .

❊ XVI ❊

W EDNESDAY AFTERNOON FRANCESCA PULLED THE BOW slowly across the strings of her violin. Beethoven. A new piece she was working on, and it was beautiful. With eyes closed, she gave herself up to the music, swaying gently back and forth. When she played music like this, nothing else in the world mattered. Only when she stopped did the problems flood back. If only she could play forever. . . .

"Well, hey, hey, hey!" said Eve, crashing through the door. "How come I've never had the honor of hearing this before?"

"Oh . . . I . . . usually play in the practice rooms at Kenner," explained Francesca, her face bright with embarrassment. She and Eve still weren't entirely comfortable around each other, even though they'd been living together for almost three weeks now. "But I just had to hear this piece again before going off to class. It's so wonderful."

"It sure ain't a Willie Nelson, that's for dern sure," Eve said, putting on her hillbilly accent.

"No . . . it's Beethoven," explained Francesca.

"Impressive, but poor old Beethoven must have been having one down day when he wrote that thing. It's about as jolly as a funeral march," Eve said.

"Yeah . . . I guess so," replied Francesca absent-mindedly.

"I sure wouldn't put money on its making the charts this season," quipped Eve, running around getting her books ready for the next class.

"No . . . I guess not," said Francesca, her voice coming from miles away.

"Hey, is something the matter?" asked Eve, stopping her perpetual motion for a second and searching Francesca's soulful face.

"No . . . no . . ." hesitated Francesca. "Not really."

" 'No' I can handle," said Eve, coming over to Francesca. "Want to talk about the 'not really' part?"

Francesca smiled vacantly. "Oh, I don't know. It's really pretty silly, I guess."

"Try me," said Eve, sitting down on the edge of Francesca's bed.

Francesca squirmed uneasily. Eve was so direct, she was hard to sidestep, but, thought Francesca, maybe it was time to stop sidestepping. She was so confused about what to do with Marty. Maybe she needed another opinion. She'd tried several times to call her older sister, Beth, and talk some of it out with her, but they kept missing each other. Besides, it wasn't the same as when they could just flop down on their beds and launch into a chat. It felt kind of weird to be calling her for advice, but Francesca had never talked her big problems out with anyone else. In fact, there were some very big problems, like Damian, even her sister didn't know about.

"Troubles with Marty?" asked Eve.

Again Francesca's face went bright red. "What! . . . How did . . . ?"

"Well, it's not too hard to figure out something's going

on with you two," Eve said. "Ever since you guys got back from New York, Marty's been actually sweet to me. Okay, maybe sweet's stretching it a bit, but we haven't had one knockdown, drag-out fight in four days. He's become positively boring. I can tell he's trying to get on my good side . . . small as it is!"

Francesca laughed. "Yeah, well, I guess you could say we might be seeing each other. But," she added, more for herself than Eve, "I think it's mostly just a good friendship."

"Might be!" laughed Eve. "Mostly! Not to be confused with 'Me and My Shadow.' If what I saw these last few days keeps up, I may have to make an appointment to get even five minutes of your time."

"Geez, I'm sorry, Eve," said Francesca. "Marty just keeps turning up everywhere. Did you want to talk to me about something?"

"No, I just thought it might be fun to play roommates occasionally. You know, grab a pizza together, toss a few water balloons, stuff like that, before the year's out and we go our separate ways."

Francesca looked closely at Eve and felt a wave of guilt wash over her. She was very lucky to have such a fun person as a roommate, unlike poor Ellie, stuck with Irritable Iris. She owed Eve more consideration. Besides, they'd probably have a good time together, and it would be nice to have a break from Marty. Things were already threatening to move too fast, and she didn't know how to handle any of it.

"Okay, so what's happening with Klein?" asked Eve.

"Oh, Eve, I don't know," began Francesca.

"Well, start talking and maybe we can figure it out. When it comes to problems with boys, I consider myself a bit of an expert."

Francesca looked at her quizzically.

"Yeah, yeah," said Eve. Francesca didn't miss the defensive tone of her voice. "I know what you're thinking:

'Hotheaded little Eve Jacobson having trouble with boys! I'm surprised anyone would even go out with her.' Right?''

"Oh, Eve, no! Not at all!" gushed Francesca. "You just seem to be so up and in such control all the time, I never imagined you having any problems." Francesca restlessly plumped the pillow on her bed.

"Well, kid, shows you how wrong you can be," said Eve, back in her former flip mood. "I tell you, when my parents got divorced—"

"Divorced! I didn't know your parents were divorced," said Francesca, more overwhelmed with guilt than ever. She hadn't paid a moment's attention to Eve's problems.

"You never asked, and it's not exactly the sort of thing I want to rush around bragging about," said Eve. "It was a tough time."

"I'm sure it was," Francesca said sympathetically. "I can't imagine what it would be like if my parents got divorced."

"I just hope they never do," said Eve. "It's certainly not my idea of a good time." Suddenly she stood up and began pacing the room. "But, at any rate, when everything was going nuts at home, I started seeing this guy— Rex Anderson. I mean, would you date someone called Rex? Doesn't take too many hours of old Latin 101 to know Rex means 'king.' And this guy was convinced he was king of all, especially me! But I was so screwed up at that time, I just let him play the role, call the shots, take control. I guess I really fell for him because I needed someone . . . anyone so badly then. He was my first real boyfriend." Eve stared at the wall in silence for a second. Slowly and hesitantly Francesca stood up and put her hand on Eve's arm, hoping to communicate that she understood.

"It wasn't an easy relationship to get out of," said Eve quietly. "I'd gotten so tangled up in him, I didn't know where he ended and I started. I was incredibly physically attracted to him. It was a terrible mess. I felt like I was drowning all the time."

"But you managed to break free?" asked Francesca, still holding Eve's arm.

"Yes . . . thank goodness," said Eve, staring at the scuffed toe of her tennis shoes. "But it took me a while to feel good about relationships again. I had let Rex push me into too much. I needed time alone."

"You all right now?"

Eve laughed. "As all right as most people, I guess." She hesitated, then looked Francesca in the eye. "So, what's happening with you and Marty?"

For a moment Francesca was reluctant to answer. She was too busy thinking about Eve's admissions. Since she'd never discussed Damian with anyone before, she'd gone around all this time thinking she was the only one who didn't know how to be in a healthy, warm relationship. Her one night with Damian began to pale before Eve's difficult relationship with Rex. Eve wasn't always in control, either! Francesca felt a partial weight lift from her shoulders, and before she knew it, she and Eve were sitting cross-legged on the floor, and she was describing that night with Damian and her fears of getting close again.

When Francesca was through, much to her surprise, Eve laughed softly and knowingly.

"So you got a little hot, and Damian got hotter. Next time you'll know what's happening and you'll have more control. No big deal. Really. That's happened to everyone."

Francesca looked at Eve wide-eyed. Relief flooded through her, and for a few moments she sat in silence.

"So, what do I do about Marty?" Francesca finally asked. "I just don't know if I can deal with him. Sometimes I feel like a two-year-old. Marty and I have a great friendship. Maybe we'd ruin it if we go any further. All we've done so far is kiss a little."

"And nothing terrible happened. Right?" asked Eve. "It felt good, but you didn't feel the need to tear your clothes off, and Marty didn't suggest it. Right? You see? After that experience with Damian, you changed. You realized you have control over your life and your body. That's what I learned from Rex. Boys don't control our lives. We do."

"That's easy to say," began Francesca, "but I don't really feel that. I guess I'm kind of old-fashioned that way. I'm not used to telling boys what to do."

"Ei yie yie!" sighed Eve. "Kid, you're going to have some big problems unless you amend that real soon. Why not start with Marty?"

Francesca gave her a questioning look. "What do you mean?"

"Well, it seems to me you really like the guy a lot and would like to get to know him better, but are scared of him because of something that happened with someone else. Right?"

"Right," agreed Francesca, eager to hear Eve's advice.

"So just take it slowly with Marty and only go as far as *you* want. *You* decide what the relationship is worth and where *you* want it to go. But it would be a shame and unfair to you both to just cut it off because of Damian. Maybe it's time to really put that behind you and get on with the future."

"Yeah . . . maybe you're right," said Francesca thoughtfully. "Maybe—"

"Now, enough of this heavy stuff. Let's boogie!" said Eve, fishing under her bed and pulling out her banjo case. "I've got to get my act together for the talent show or I'll be laughed off the stage."

"You won't be the only one," said Francesca mournfully. "I had rehearsal with Sue and Iris last night and, if it's possible, it went worse than the first one. They just don't seem to be interested anymore."

"Did you talk to them about it?" Eve asked. "I mean, tell 'em you were kind of concerned about how it was going."

"I . . . I tried," replied Francesca. "But Iris isn't the easiest person to get through to."

"That's for sure," agreed Eve. "What are you going to do about it, then?"

"Hope for a miracle, I guess. We've got one more rehearsal. Maybe they just like to leave things till the last minute," Francesca said. "The whole thing is sure giving me a bad case of nerves, though."

"I bet," Eve said. "Makes me glad I'm doing a one-woman show. I'm going to have fun with it."

"That's one of the good things about being a directing student. You can get up there and do anything you want. You're really not competing with anyone like the rest of us, who are supposed to be actors and singers. If Iris and Sue blow it for me, then my whole reputation here is down the tubes." Francesca suddenly felt queasier than ever.

"Well, if I were you, I'd just lay it on the line at the next rehearsal; tell 'em you want out if it doesn't go well," said Eve.

"The next rehearsal is the day of the show." Francesca sighed miserably. "I'm going to practice my part on my own, but there's not much I can do if we sound terrible together."

Eve shook her head. "Iris is some piece of work, huh?" Francesca grimaced.

"Look, before you totally flip out, grab your violin for a sec. Ever play bluegrass fiddle?"

"Bluegrass fiddle?!" giggled Francesca, glad for the chance to forget her problems for a little while. "No, I never have!"

Eve quickly tuned up her banjo and slipped on her picks. "Look, I'm going to play something simple . . . key of C . . . okay? You follow."

Without giving Francesca a chance to protest, Eve launched into a high-flying, foot-stomping, skirt-twirling piece of bluegrass. At first Francesca couldn't imagine keeping up, but as she listened, she quickly picked up the tune and was soon sawing away on her violin.

"We're hot!" shouted Eve, finishing the song up with a flourish of fast notes. Francesca burst out laughing and fell back on her bed.

"And that's our big problem, in more ways than one!"

✻ XVII ✻

FRANCESCA DRAGGED HERSELF SLOWLY UP THE STAIRS TO Iris's room Friday, late afternoon. Well, this was it. Final rehearsal for the talent show. Why Iris had switched it to the last minute like this, she couldn't figure out. If anything was wrong, they had no time to fix it. The curtain went up in just under four hours. The programs had already been printed and stuck under everyone's door right after lunch. Her act with Iris and Sue was listed simply as, "Ensemble Number." Even that was strange. Why hadn't Iris told them it was an ensemble number from *A Chorus Line* and give it its right title? Francesca suddenly realized she'd left too much up to Iris in this whole thing. But it was one thing for Eve to tell her to put her foot down and take some of the control away from Iris, and another matter altogether to actually do it. Iris had control worked out to a fine art. With Marty it had been easier. He actually seemed to want her to have a say in what they did. After her talk with Eve, Francesca told Marty about her fears, and he'd made it completely clear that both of their needs counted. Not just his. If she needed room, fine. He needed space, too. And that was fine with her, though

Francesca was aware that the moment he expressed his desire for independence, she suddenly felt a little funny. Jealous even. But mostly the conversation felt wonderful . . . unlike the prospects of the talent show.

Taking a deep breath, Francesca knocked on Iris's door, which seemed to set off a flurry of nervous activity on the other side. Francesca was about to knock again when the door was flung open.

Francesca could not believe her eyes. She was sure, in fact, that she was dreaming.

"Taaa Daaaaaaa!" exclaimed Iris. She and Sue stood before Francesca wearing nothing but flesh-colored leotards with painted-on bright red G-strings and bras. Iris had a string of battery-powered flashing lights strung around her shapely hips.

Francesca's mouth dropped open. She stared at the girls in horror.

"See, she loves it already," said Iris, smiling wickedly at Sue. "I told you she would."

"Wha . . . what . . . are you doing?" gasped Francesca, feeling her knees threatening to crumble. The outfits were disgusting.

"Come in, Frannie," said Iris, taking Francesca's arm and leading her inside before she could protest. The door clicked shut behind them. "Now then, Frannie, I guess it didn't take much to notice our act from *A Chorus Line* wasn't getting anywhere. I mean, any fool could see that. We just weren't simpatico."

"But . . . I . . . liked it," protested Francesca feebly.

"Yes, I know you did, but Sue and I just couldn't get into it, could we, Sue?" Iris said. "We would have really blown it for you, and there's a lot riding on this first talent show, you know."

Francesca nodded dumbly. She knew she was standing in the middle of a nightmare, but didn't have a clue how to escape.

"It was too dry. No pizzazz," continued Iris, clearly enjoying Francesca's discomfort. "So we've come up with a new number—the bump-and-grind scene from *Gypsy*—'You Got to Have a Gimmick.' You know it, I'm sure."

Francesca was too stunned to do anything but nod.

"Well, no . . . no, don't worry," rattled on Iris, misinterpreting Francesca's worried look. "It's short and zippy. Really perfect. Won't take long to learn at all. Here, put this on and we'll run through it." Iris threw Francesca a leotard, and with mock politeness, averted her eyes.

Francesca felt like a cornered rat. She stared from the leotard to the door to the window, trying to think up some way to escape. The scene Iris had picked might be perfect for Iris, but it was disaster for her. Three strippers explaining the gimmicks they use to make them special to their customers. A violent shudder ripped through Francesca. Slowly and reluctantly she slipped into the leotard, cringing at the feel of the slippery, tight fabric against her skin.

"Iris . . . I can't do this," began Francesca, catching sight of herself in Iris's mirror. The leotard really left the impression she had nothing on except the G-string.

"Why, Frannie, I can't understand why not. You're an actress, aren't you? You should be able to take on any role that's thrown at you. At least, if you're planning on being a decent actress one day, that is."

Again Francesca was stunned into silence. Iris was right . . . in a way. One of the reasons she'd come to SPAR was to expand her repertoire. At Newton High she was typecast as kind of the eternal Flying Nun. This role from *Gypsy* would certainly put her to the test, show her if she could really act, because there was nothing inside her that had any sympathy with the role. It would be acting in the purest sense. She glanced at the lines for the scene. At least it was a fairly short one. She'd be able to get up and down fast.

They spent the next hour running through the song a few

times. Francesca felt sicker and sicker as the minutes ticked by. When finally it was time to break for dinner, Francesca was completely unable to eat. Totally overwhelmed, she slipped her pants and shirt over the costume and started for her room.

"Oh, Frannie," Iris called out, as she reached her door. "Be careful with that outfit. We don't want it to get messed up before curtain time!"

Francesca shut the door behind her and sank to the floor, drawing her knees up to her chest. This was going to be one of the longest nights of her life. Idly she studied her lines, but was unable to concentrate. Or was it just plain unwillingness? Francesca couldn't think of a song she'd rather do less.

The hours moved by quickly—too quickly—and then it was time to go. She wrapped her raincoat securely round her and joined the flow of kids headed for Kenner. Some were in costume, some had musical instruments, some looked serious, and most looked like this was a great big joke. Francesca knew she looked scared . . . pure and simple.

"Wait up, Francesca," came a familiar voice. Francesca turned and saw Ellie hurrying down the hall toward her.

"Let me guess," said Ellie, eyeing Francesca's raincoat mischievously. "You're doing the water scene from *Singin' in the Rain.* Right?"

"I wish," replied Francesca dismally. "Would you believe a bump-and-grind scene from *Gypsy?*"

"You're not. . . . No, you can't possibly be," stammered Ellie, looking somewhat horrified. "I thought you were doing that thing from *A Chorus Line!?* What happened?"

"Iris Setlow, that's what," sighed Francesca. "She and Sue just weren't into that scene, so they switched it this morning. I'm Mazeppa!"

"The one who has to 'bump it with a trumpet'?!" exclaimed Ellie.

"Exactly," said Francesca, feeling worse and worse. "And if you want to get really depressed, take a look at this costume." She held open her raincoat for a second so Ellie could get a quick look.

"Oh, my gosh!" said Ellie in shock, then smashed her fist angrily into her palm. "Damn that slimy snake! Don't you see what she's trying to do?"

Francesca shook her head in confusion. "No. . . . What do you mean?"

"Oh, Francesca, Iris has your ticket. She knows that scene would be the last thing you'd ever pick. That's why she bamboozled you into it."

"I think I'm missing something," said Francesca. "What ticket?"

"Hell, Francesca, are you really that naive? Iris wants to embarrass you . . . wants you to make a fool of yourself. Can't you see that?"

"But . . . why?" pleaded Francesca, her dark eyes widening. "What have I done to her?"

"You exist. You're gorgeous, and don't think Iris has missed the looks the entire male population of SPAR has been giving you. She can't stand it." Ellie giggled. "Personally, I love it—the way she seethes when you walk by."

"But I don't want an enemy," said Francesca honestly. "There's no need for Iris to hate me."

"Go look in the mirror, kid, and you'll see the only reason Iris Setlow needs. You're her competition, and I think she knows who's going to win, hands down."

"Oh, I hope that's not true," said Francesca softly, her face awash in consternation.

"Frannie, honey, there you are," gushed Iris, bearing down on the two girls when they got backstage. "I thought you were going to let me down, and I tell you, I think we three girls are going to steal the show."

Francesca opened her mouth to protest, but Iris bowled right over her.

"I got Zed to change us to the second slot. Amy Landow's going first. Playing some ballad she wrote herself. Thought our act would have even more impact if we followed something slow and mushy like that. Break a leg, Frannie." Iris swept away before Francesca could get a word in edgewise. She looked desperately over at Ellie, who started to say something but was interrupted by the first act being announced.

There was a buzz of excitement in the room that slowly quieted down when a slender, petite girl walked self-consciously up onstage and perched on a stool. She rested her guitar on her knee and strummed a few chords to check its tuning.

"Looks like Sissy Spacek, doesn't she?" whispered Ellie.

"She really does," Francesca agreed. And she did. She had the same shy smile and the same wheat-colored hair hanging loosely around her face. She even had freckles and pale, cornflower-blue eyes. Now, if she could act as well as Spacek did, they were all going to be in deep trouble, Francesca thought to herself. Well, nothing like a high standard to keep them all slaving away.

"I didn't feel much like acting tonight," began Amy, lightly strumming a few simple chords while she talked. "I'm probably just as scared as anybody else here about this year ahead of us."

A rumbling of nervous giggles washed through the assembly. People grinned sheepishly at each other, although Francesca, looking around backstage, noticed that C.J. didn't blink an eye or twitch a muscle. He seemed to be miles away, as usual. Amy continued talking in her soothing Midwest accent.

"I'm from Missouri and I don't know if you folks keep up with us way out there in farmland, U.S.A., but we've been having some real serious problems lately. Lot of people are losing their farms 'cause they can't make enough money farming anymore to pay the mortgages." She hit a louder, dissonant chord, then fell back to the quiet strumming before continuing. "So . . . in honor of all the people out there in Missouri—my friends—who are facing these tough times, I dedicate this song; it's one I wrote myself."

By the end of the first stanza, Francesca had tears in her eyes. Amy's voice was high and convincing, her song beautiful—a story of pride and loss, of the death of the American farm and its honorable way of life.

"Oh, Ellie, I can't possibly get up and do that horrible scene after that magnificent song," sniffled Francesca when the final words of the song drifted down over the crowd like autumn leaves. There was silence for a moment, then thunderous applause. "It would be sacrilege."

"Come with me," said Ellie, taking Francesca firmly by the arm. Francesca stumbled after her down a flight of back stairs. They almost ran headlong into Iris and Sue.

"Ready, Frannie?" cooed Iris, the malicious glint in her eye convincing Francesca that Ellie was probably right about Iris's cruel intentions. She swallowed hard.

"Here's your trumpet," gushed Iris, handing Francesca a cardboard cutout. "Remember to really bump and grind, girls. Let's stand this place on its ear."

Francesca felt her face go bright red.

"Sorry, Iris," interrupted Ellie smoothly, "but I'm afraid you're going to have to go on without Francesca. She's just received word from home. Bad news." Ellie put her arm protectively around Francesca's shoulders. Francesca didn't know what she was up to, but she trusted Ellie and played along, putting a sad, faraway look on her face and leaning heavily on Ellie's arm.

"But . . . But . . . the show has to go on. What'll I do?" babbled Iris.

"I'm sure a great actress like you can handle both roles," said Ellie. "Now, if you'll excuse us, I was just helping Francesca back to the dorm. I don't think she should be alone at a time like this."

Francesca had to hold her breath to keep from giggling. Ellie was putting on one amazing performance. Forcefully keeping her face wreathed in sadness, Francesca distractedly handed the trumpet back to Iris. Iris stared at it dumbfounded, for once completely speechless. Ellie led Francesca dramatically away.

They just managed to make their way secretively to the other side of backstage before they collapsed into giggles.

"Oh, I loved it," laughed Ellie. "Just loved it. Did you see her face?"

"It was almost as red as her G-string," replied Francesca. "She was burning."

"Seething," shot back Ellie. "I'd say she was seething."

"You think she knew we were pulling her leg?" asked Francesca, her eyes brimming over with the tears of laughter.

"Of course she did. Iris might be a pain, but she's no dummy," said Ellie. "What are the chances of you getting bad news from home just at this moment? Zero, I'd say!"

"Good point," said Francesca. "What do you think she's going to do to us? I doubt if someone like Iris will see the humor in all this."

"Well," said Ellie, sinking her hands deep into her pockets, "I don't really care. As far as I'm concerned, I have officially declared war on Iris Setlow."

Their giggles were interrupted by the announcement that the next act would not be performed, so the show would go on with the third act, a song by C.J. Rollings.

"I'm going to have to explain this to Zed," Francesca whispered.

"Tell him you got the flu, and make sure you sign up for the next contest. Just be sure it's a solo act!" Again they cracked up.

"Shhh . . . Let's listen to this," whispered Ellie, moving over to a crack in the curtain. "I'd like to see what C.J.'s all about. He can't be all slime."

"I know what you mean," agreed Francesca, joining Ellie. "Honestly, I get the feeling there is more to him than he lets on."

As Francesca settled down to watch, a strong feeling of excitement engulfed her. She'd been spared a real humiliation. And she could tell she was ready to translate her growing ability to "get close" into her craft. Lilly's next class was only days away. . . .

C.J. jumped when Zed called out his name. His turn already! What happened? He was supposed to follow Iris, not Amy. As he heard Zed explain that there would be no second act after all, he could feel his heart start to beat double-time. Every seat in the theater was full. All the kids from SPAR were there, waiting for him to get up onstage.

Suddenly he was afraid he wouldn't be able to move. Life had been so crazy lately, he hadn't really had time to practice much. He just wasn't ready. Maybe the second act had a good idea. Canceling out was a fine option. His only option. C.J. turned around, about to approach Zed, when he heard a voice coming from deep inside himself.

"You have talent. When are you going to prove it to yourself? WHEN!?"

Suddenly C.J. squared his shoulders. If he didn't see this through, he wasn't sure he'd ever get up onstage again. It was now or never. His father had convinced him it was his talent that got him to SPAR; now it was up to C.J. to prove his father right.

C.J. took a deep breath and walked slowly up the stairs

to the stage. It seemed extra big being up there all alone. There weren't even any props. Just a big, empty stage. C.J. coughed nervously and adjusted the mike.

"I . . . uh . . . I'm going to sing a song from the show *Company*. A favorite of mine. Called 'Being Alive.' "

C.J. adjusted the mike and cleared his throat. The pianist in the orchestra pit played the introduction. Finally C.J. knew there was nothing left to do but open his mouth and sing . . . which he did. The words flowed out, hesitantly at first, but after the first line, the song took over and C.J. could feel himself get lost in it as he did every time he sang this song. His deep rich tenor filled the auditorium, begging the audience to make him come alive, to give him someone who would make him care.

For the first time, C.J. realized why he loved this song so much. It reminded him of himself. Maybe he'd never been brave enough to see that before. But the words spoke to him now as never before. He was getting tired of one-night stands. He was ready to make a commitment to someone, to share with someone, to give to someone.

The song soared into the final crescendo, its desperate plea hanging in the still air for a long, silent moment at the end. Then the place broke up with wild applause. C.J. let his breath out with a rush and smiled his thanks to the audience. He didn't know how to describe it, but he felt in his heart he'd just made a major breakthrough with himself and his peers.

Suddenly his eye caught Serena's and his smile faded. Her blue eyes were filled with adoration, staring up at him with an emotion he didn't want to recognize.

But he knew he'd have to . . . sooner or later. Serena clearly thought he'd been singing to her—begging her to love him, to make him care. Only, Serena was wrong. He'd sung "Being Alive" for a girl he'd not yet met. She was out there somewhere, and he was determined to find her.

Serena was not in the running, and at some point C.J. realized he'd have to let her know. But not now. He was too happy. Later, he thought. She's too delicious to leave quite yet. . . . Later, much later . . .

✳ XVIII ✳

DID THE AIR SEEM SWEETER? THE SUN BRIGHTER? Francesca thought so as she practically skipped down the path to Kenner Monday morning. The whole world seemed better, and certainly more under control since her talk with Eve. Even the Iris fiasco seemed unimportant now. How lucky she was to have such a wonderful roommate . . . and how lucky to have someone like Marty interested in her. Eve was right. It would be dumb to break things off now, just when she and Marty were getting to really know each other. She owed it to herself to let things run their course. If nothing else, they'd have a wonderful friendship.

Francesca cut through the rhododendron bushes behind Kenner. She didn't want to be late for her voice interpretation class, and she could save a few seconds by not walking around to the front doors.

"Oh, I'm sorry," she stammered, blundering into a clearing and almost running smack into C.J. wrapped around a girl she didn't know. Francesca looked at C.J. curiously. Hadn't he and Serena been seeing each other pretty steadily? What's going on? Francesca thought.

"Hey, no problem," said C.J., not bothering to release

the girl who was now staring at him adoringly. "We're just learning to express emotion. Right, Trish?"

Francesca hurried by them and slid into her seat several seconds after the bell rang. This was the fourth time the class had met, but it still made her nervous. Francesca cleared her throat and stared at the ceiling, willing herself to remain calm. Lilly had not suggested duets since that first class, but Francesca knew it was only a matter of time. And the moment she glanced at the sheet music resting on the desk before her, Francesca knew the moment had arrived. "We Kiss in the Shadow" was a love song from *The King and I,* and it had two parts.

What have I learned in the two weeks since Lilly and I had our talk, she asked herself over and over. A list began to form in her mind. She'd tried to open herself up more. Look at her talk with Eve. And things were going well and were going to get even better with Marty. She thought of Damian, but already after her talk with Eve, it was like looking at an old photograph of someone who meant something then, but not now—something too far in the past to be a part of current life. The pain was going, fading out like the edges of the old photo. Francesca felt her body begin to relax. A lot had changed. She understood herself a little better, and somehow reaching out to people had become wonderful—not frightening.

Francesca felt her tension begin to melt into excitement. And then the class got under way.

Francesca shot Theodore a big grin when they were called to the front. Francesca knew "We Kiss in the Shadow," well. It was a beautiful song about illicit lovers meeting on the sly. Very passionate and moving. Thinking of the intimate words, a momentary flash of uncertainty descended, but Francesca fought it off. She could do it. She could be convincing. Francesca took a deep breath and listened intently while the pianist played the introduction, her mind in a whirl. She was an actress playing the part of

Tuptim. No . . . she *was* Tuptim. The words, the emotions were hers, not Francesca Minelli's. It was up to Francesca Minelli to convince everyone of that.

When the introduction ended, Francesca turned to face Theodore. He *was* Lun Tha. She could see it. She could feel it. The man she loved but couldn't have. They locked eyes and began to sing. The words poured from Francesca's heart and soul, her sweet soprano weaving in and out of Theodore's deep tones. A tear trickled down her face. Tuptim and Lun Tha embraced, then pulled apart, aware in the final moment of what would never be theirs, aware of the great, tragic loss.

Silence descended at the end of the song. Not a chair squeaked, not a person coughed. Utter silence.

Lilly began to clap, and moments later the whole class joined in. Francesca smiled at them through her tears. She could do it! She was going to make it! Her heart soared with a new sense of happiness, a new sense of self. Anything was possible!

"Francesca?" called Serena, running to catch up with her on the steps of Kenner. Francesca was still flying high from her success in class, but tried to bring herself down to earth when she saw Serena's troubled face.

"What is it?" she asked, wondering if Serena's oversize sweater was going to slip all the way down her chest or continue to magically hang off her shoulder like that.

"Have you seen C.J.? I've just got to find him."

Francesca looked closely at Serena's face. The girl was in love! Serena had completely fallen for C.J.! How could she? And what was Francesca supposed to tell her: Yes, she'd seen C.J. out in the bushes with another girl! Francesca's head went into overdrive.

"C.J.? . . . uh . . ." she stammered.

"Yes," cried Serena. "He promised to meet me in the cafeteria before last period, and didn't show. Oh, I just hope nothing's happened to him. He's so reckless, you know.''

With everything, including your emotions, it seems, thought Francesca, almost telling Serena about C.J. and Trish. But Serena looked so lost and in love, she couldn't bring her that pain. Serena was going to have to find out for herself. Like she had with Damian, like Eve had with Rex. There were some things you just couldn't tell people.

''No . . . no . . . I haven't seen him recently,'' replied Francesca, only telling a half lie.

As she watched Serena run off, stopping another couple farther along the path, a dark feeling began to envelop Francesca. What if Marty treated her like C.J. treated Serena? What if she fell in love with him? Would she really be able to control things if she got more involved? Maybe she should call it quits before things got too crazy. Maybe, but was that really what she wanted? No. Yes. No. She didn't know what she thought anymore. A shudder raced through Francesca's body as she slowly climbed the hill back to the dorm.

No one is going to hurt me, she thought. Whatever I have to do to make sure of that, I'll do.

About the Author

Simone Nicholas is a talented veteran of the Broadway stage. She has acted and danced her way through seven hit musicals and countless off-Broadway productions. She currently serves as an artistic consultant for a national program for youth in the arts. This is her first novel.